Lavender Sky

Denise Janette Bruneau

ISBN 978-1-64349-292-6 (paperback)
ISBN 978-1-64349-293-3 (digital)

Christian Faith Publishing, Inc.
832 Park Avenue
Meadville, PA 16335
www.christianfaithpublishing.com

Printed in the United States of America

Dear Reader,

Thank you for deciding to read this story. While *Lavender Sky* is a fictional story, it is based on a true story of love, redemption, and hope. This book is dedicated to Heather, who had amazing courage at a very important time in her life. I want to especially thank my husband, Mark, for his support for my writing. Thank you to my Aunt Cherie for the time she took to edit my story. I thank God for giving me the desire to write and, through my writing, share a little bit of His love with my readers.

Blessings to you and your family,
Denise

Prologue

◆◆◆◆◆◆◆◆◆◆

October 1989

Eighteen-year-old Delaney Bartlett stood on the sidewalk as she held up the directions in her hand. She frowned as she looked back and forth from the directions to the building. *This can't be it*, she thought. The dilapidated structure appeared to be outdated and abandoned. She glanced down at the address again and read it out loud, as if it might change the words on the paper, "234 E. Broadway." She exhaled and she looked up toward the building again. There was no mistake. This was it.

She could feel her heart sink as she surveyed the building. The red brick exterior was worn. There were cracks and holes in the mortar and several remnants of bricks had fallen off and crumbled. Two of the front windows displayed large cracks, and one window was missing part of the glass, where it looked as if someone had thrown a rock through it. Delaney walked down the brick pathway to the front door. The pathway bricks were overgrown with weeds sprouting up between them. She stopped as she approached the entrance door. She took a long, deep breath as if she was contemplating leaving. Finally, with cautious effort, she stepped forward and pushed the door open.

She hesitated as she peered through the door. Her imagination started to run wild, as she imagined a ghost jumping out at her in the dark. When she could see no movement from inside, she opened the door wider and stepped in. The heavy, rusted, steel door slammed behind her as she let it go. The loud boom caused her to duck her head as if she was dodging a bullet. She recovered from the noise, but her heart pounded loudly as if it had jumped out of her rib cage. She stood in the dingy corridor trying to catch her breath. It was quiet, and the only noise she could hear was her own breathing. Darkness surrounded her with only a little light shining from a light bulb dangling from the ceiling. She didn't move, as the hair on the back of her neck stood up, and she eyed her surroundings. In front of her, a wood staircase stared back at her and appeared to lead directly upward into a dark abyss. The stairs were worn and dirty and appeared to have been traveled well. There was one door on each side of the corridor, with each one leading to an old, abandoned office space. A "For Lease" sign was propped against each door.

"Who would actually rent this space?" she mumbled under her breath. As she made her way toward the steps, she noticed a sign on the wall. It was handwritten with black, faded ink and read, "Clinic." Below the sign was an arrow drawn on the wall pointing up the weathered stairs. Her heart began to race again, and she could feel her palms sweating. She felt frozen as she stared up the dark stairs and wondered if she could go through with her plan. She had reviewed her options many times, and this seemed like her only path. It didn't change the way she felt, though. Despite her careful planning and resignation, she still wanted to run in the other direction. She stood in the silent, dark corridor for several minutes contemplating her decision again. She stared down at the floor, trying to remember to breathe. Finally, she shook her head back and forth, pursed her lips, and took a step forward.

As she ascended the stairwell, her legs felt like heavy weights. Halfway up the stairs, her foot missed a step, and she fell forward catching herself on her knees. She was shaking as she looked up from the darkness on her knees. Feeling afraid, she started to utter a prayer, but her guilt drowned out any words. She stood up and carefully continued up the stairs, one step at a time. When she reached the top of the stairwell, it was so dark she could barely make out the words on a door sign directly in front of her. She leaned in closer to the sign and read "Clinic."

Delaney slowly pushed the door open. There wasn't much light in the room, as she peered through the half-open door. She opened the door further, and the lighting improved. She was surprised to see many young women packed into a waiting room. She stepped into the room and felt a sudden heaviness, as if she could feel the weight of thirty pairs of eyes on her. The air felt thick, as she tried to take a deep breath. The room was so quiet that even the slightest sounds seemed amplified.

There wasn't enough seating, and some women were sitting on the floor, while others were leaning against the walls. The waiting room was dingy and old, and the musty smell made her stomach turn. The floor was covered with orange shag carpet that appeared to be from the 1960s, and the plaster walls and ceiling had cracks throughout. There were no pictures on the walls, just several nail holes, where pictures might have once hung. Delaney made her way past the women to the reception desk.

"Sign in," the lady said without expression from behind the desk. She handed Delaney a clipboard with several papers attached and, without looking at her, said, "Fill out each form completely, sign the consents, and then bring them back to me."

She looked at the lady for a moment, hopeful for some kind of greeting, but the lady didn't make eye contact with her. Delaney lowered her head and turned around. She surveyed the room and finally spotted an empty space on the wall. There, she leaned on the wall, wishing she could disappear into it. She filled out the forms one by one. As she reached the pages of consents, her heart began to thump hard in her chest. She read over the risks: bleeding, infection, death … death? No one had mentioned that possibility to her, though today, she'd almost rather die than have to make this choice.

She felt lightheaded and sunk down against the wall onto her bottom. She sighed heavily and looked around her. Despite the crowded room, Delaney felt more alone right now than she'd ever felt. She paused to ponder her decision for another moment, as if hoping a different and better solution would magically come to her. With no such luck, however, she looked down at the consents. Her eyes fought hard to hold back the erupting tears. Then, as if waving a white flag of defeat, she surrendered and signed on the dotted lines. She stood slowly with a heavy heart and legs, waiting for another moment of dizziness to pass. Then she drudged back toward the reception desk and handed the signed forms to the lady.

"Have a seat, and we'll call you back when we're ready for you," said the lady at the desk. She still did not look up at Delaney.

As Delaney waited for her name to be called, she glanced around the room. The other women were glancing around the same way; all of them appeared to be guarded, scared, and sad. She could feel judgment in the stare of each woman, though each look was brief. She couldn't help but wonder what circumstance had brought each one of them to this place. She felt a shared, kindred spirit of sadness and hopelessness with all of them. But there was something else. She could feel a much stronger, but subdued, emotion among the women. It was shame. Shame was flooding the room, though each face tried to disguise it. All of the eyes looked downtrodden, the mouths were without any hint of a smile, and the faces reflected despair.

"D. Bartlett," a nurse called, peeking from behind a door opening into the small waiting room.

Delaney stepped forward and locked eyes with the nurse for one second. The nurse waved her toward the open door, and Delaney followed her.

"Stand on here," she said as she pointed to a scale. The nurse then proceeded to check her vital signs. "Are you allergic to anything?"

"No," Delaney answered.

"Follow me," she ordered. Delaney followed the nameless nurse into a locker room. "This is your locker where you can lock up your belongings," the nurse said. Then, she asked, "Did you bring a robe?"

Delaney answered, "Yes."

The nurse handed her a gown that Delaney guessed was a hospital gown and said, "Change into this and then put on your robe. You can leave your socks on. Leave a urine sample in the bathroom. Write your name and date of birth on the cup with this pen. When you're dressed, go through this door and have a seat. Wait for your name to be called. Be sure to bring your payment with you."

Delaney did as the nurse instructed. She robotically changed, left a urine sample, locked her belongings in the locker, and then went through the doorway. In the next room, there was a waiting area. It was a little less stark than the first waiting room, but it still felt cold and sterile. There were some old couches scattered about, and Delaney found a place to sit on one of them. The air was still thick and musty. She peered at the women seated around her just briefly. No one was talking or making any noise. The silence was uncomfortable.

As in the other waiting room, the walls were bare without hanging pictures or posters. There were no magazines or books to read. There was no copy of a Holy Bible to read, as she had seen in many other waiting rooms, though she knew why. Everyone just sat quietly looking at the floor. Occasionally, two women would exchange an awkward, short glance and then quickly look away.

After an hour, Delaney heard her name called. "D. Bartlett." It was a different lady this time, and she wasn't wearing medical scrubs.

Delaney stood up and followed her into her office.

"Have a seat," the lady said.

Delaney sat down in a chair across from the lady's desk. A nameplate on the desktop read, "Jane Smith, Counselor."

"My name is Jane, and we need to start today by discussing a few details," Jane said with a poker face. She continued without looking at Delaney, "The first matter of business today is payment. You owe $273.00 for this procedure. How do you want to pay for this?"

Delaney pulled her only credit card from her robe pocket and handed it to Jane. Jane took the card and ran it. There was an awkward moment of silence as the card had to be run a second time. Delaney held her breath. What if her card was declined? If she couldn't pay, she imagined she'd be kicked out in a heartbeat. *Heartbeat,* the word crossed through her mind almost reaching her heart, and then, the machine beeped with approval, bringing Delaney's thoughts back to the business at hand. Jane handed back her card.

"Okay, well, sign here. Now, we need to talk about the procedure," she said. "Are you sure this is what you want to do—" Jane started to ask and then glanced at the folder on the desk to be reminded of Delaney's name. She continued, ". . . Delaney?"

Delaney felt flushed and started to sweat as she signed the credit card receipt. She looked at Jane wanting to say, *No,* but answered, "Yes."

Jane asked, "Have you talked to your parents about this?"

Delaney felt a wave of nausea and a shock of horror go through her at the same time. She stammered, "No, no, my mom passed away. And my dad, well, he can never know. He would be so disappointed in me ... and embarrassed."

That answer seemed good enough for Jane, since she did not try to talk her out of it or offer any alternatives. She replied, "Okay, then, have a seat back in the waiting room, and we'll call you when we're ready for you." That was the extent of her counseling session.

Delaney sat and waited for nearly two hours. Several times, she thought she might get up and run out. But her resolve had gotten her this far, and somehow, her bottom stayed planted in her seat. Despite her fear and uncertainty, she couldn't see another way out. There was no way she could explain this to anyone without being penalized in some way. Her dad was vested in her future and paying for her education. She was studying to be a chemical engineer, which she didn't love, but it was a respectable major. If she walked out now, she'd have to change the course of her life. She'd probably have to drop out of college. She even worried that her dad would love her less if he knew she was pregnant and had to leave school.

Delaney's thoughts were interrupted as she heard her name called. Her stomach turned, and she thought she might vomit. The wave of nausea passed, but her stomach still felt heavy. She stood after a moment but couldn't feel her legs. A lump swelled in her throat, and her thoughts started racing. It was time. After a moment, she could feel her legs again, and she stepped forward, though she wasn't sure if they would support her. She followed the nurse through a set of swinging, double doors.

"Take off your robe and hang it here," the nurse said pointing to a hook on the wall. "I'll make sure you get it back before you go home today."

Delaney complied without saying anything.

"Go ahead and sit on the stretcher. Put your feet up and get under the covers. I'm going to do an ultrasound, and then, I'm going to start an IV in your arm."

Delaney did as she was told. The stretcher was a skinny bed with wheels and arm rails. The nurse pulled a large ultrasound machine up next to the stretcher. She squeezed cold gel onto Delaney's lower abdomen, and the coldness felt like a bite to her skin. The nurse proceeded to place a handheld device on Delaney's abdomen, pushing it and moving it at different angles. She appeared to be looking at a screen and typing in data. At one point, the screen was almost in Delaney's visual field, and Delaney strained to see the picture. The nurse noticed her mistake and quickly reached up to direct the screen out of Delaney's sight. She finished the ultrasound and then moved to sit on a stool at Delaney's side.

"Hold out your arm," the nurse demanded.

Delaney held her arm out, and the nurse placed a tourniquet around her upper arm. It was tight.

"Make a fist and squeeze," the nurse said with the tone of a military sergeant. Delaney complied, feeling as if she might be in trouble if she didn't obey right away. The nurse said nothing else as she started the IV. There was no small talk. There was nothing.

"Keep your arms inside the rails," the nurse said with her commanding tone. Then, she wheeled Delaney back to an operating room.

Delaney had never been in an operating room, but she assumed that this was it. It was frigid and sterile-looking, though it also smelled musty. She surmised that the walls and ceiling had once been white, but years without a fresh coat of paint had made them look dingy yellow. Her eyes caught a glimpse of red fluid on the off-white tile floor.

She panicked as she took a double take and thought, *Wait, was that blood?*

Delaney's heart began to race faster. *Blood?* She thought again, *Maybe this was a really bad mistake.* She started to feel as if she was having a panic attack.

"I'm going to place this mask over your face, and you should become more relaxed," said a man's voice from above her head.

Her breath had become shallow and rapid, and she started to feel like she couldn't breathe. Once the mask was placed over her face, however, her anxiety lessened. She had the slight realization that she had been given some kind of relaxing medication. Time seemed to slow down, and she felt like she was in a tunnel. The voices in the room seemed distant and muffled. She blinked her eyes several times as she started to feel sleepy. Then, she saw a man in blue scrubs and a surgery hat and mask walk into the room.

"Is that the doctor?" She tried to ask from under the mask.

She heard the man say, "We have another young one," and then, everything went black.

Delaney awoke to tearing pain in her lower abdomen. The cramping was severe, and the spasms were almost too much for her to bear. She curled up into the fetal position on the stretcher and groaned in pain, but she wasn't allowed to lie there.

The surgery nurse spoke in a commanding voice as she motioned to a chair, "Young lady, you have to get up. Go sit in that chair until the cramping gets better. Then, go to your locker and get dressed. Here are your instructions. You may leave after that. Have someone pick you up."

The chair was nothing more than a plastic table chair one might find in a library or school. It was hard and cold on her bottom and legs. The nurse handed Delaney some papers and then walked off without saying anything else.

Delaney sat in the chair with overwhelming fear. She felt dizzy, and the cramping was the worst pain she had ever felt. She couldn't help but groan as the pain wouldn't ease. As the anesthetic effect wore off, the reality of the situation began to set in. Tears erupted as she realized she had gone through with it. She began to sob, and she couldn't stop sobbing, even when the physical pain had mostly subsided.

After about an hour, Delaney was feeling more awake, and her pain had become tolerable. She slowly stood from the chair, making sure that her legs would hold her. She looked around and could see several other girls sitting in similar chairs, who appeared to be as groggy as she had been just a few minutes earlier. She had a sudden urge to escape. She walked back to her locker and opened it. She noticed that her robe had been placed back in her locker. She quickly dressed and gathered her things. Then, she reached for her robe, but stopped. She no longer wanted it, though she wasn't sure why. She left it there, turned, and left through the door she came in.

She walked home since her college apartment was only one mile from the clinic. She stepped inside her apartment, closed the door, and leaned back on it. She closed her eyes. The weight of the quietness surrounding her was heavy, and she suddenly felt overwhelmed. She wanted to talk to someone, but this secret had to stay a secret. She tried to busy herself, as she cleaned up the kitchen dishes from the night before. She felt something new in her gut, but she couldn't identify it. She flipped on the TV, hoping the sound would lessen the feeling. Then, she showered hoping that she could wash away the feeling. After her shower, she sat on her bed for a moment, hoping for a stillness to set in. The hollow sensation in the pit of her stomach only grew. She didn't like the feeling. It was heavy, nauseating, and starting to take her breath away. She had to keep moving.

She stood up and walked into the kitchen, taking an inventory of her feelings. She still felt groggy from the anesthesia, but that wasn't it. She wasn't hungry or thirsty. She was tired, but not too bad. Her physical pain was gone. She should feel some relief now. So why did she feel worse? After all, no one knew about this.

She and Jack had been a couple for nearly six months. He had persuaded her that he loved her and that she was the woman he wanted to marry after they graduated from college. Delaney had believed him. As soon as she had told him about the pregnancy, he had stood up and walked straight out the door saying, "It's not mine." She hadn't seen or heard from him since then. It still stung so much to think about it. She had loved him and given herself completely to him. Jack had made her feel stupid and naïve. Her dad had warned her about him, but she had believed her dad wasn't giving Jack a chance. She knew she could never tell her dad about this. He would be so disappointed and angry.

She had planned this out perfectly, and no one knew about it. She had survived it, and she was done. Or was she? Something had happened that she hadn't expected. It hadn't been as straightforward as she thought it would be. It was true that the day and the procedure had gone without an event, but something major had changed. Something was still growing inside of her despite the removal a life. It was an emptiness coming from deep inside, from her soul, and it was unmistakable. A moment of clarity swept over her as she realized the depth of her actions. She had not only allowed but also signed up for the loss of a human life, her own child.

It was six o'clock when she looked out her kitchen window for sunlight. She had expected to find some comfort in the sunset. Instead, the sky had taken on an eerie green hue, and the clouds had become gray and threatening. Thunder bellowed in the distance. She felt the implication of the stormy sky paralleling the reality of what she had done, and her heart began to ache. She realized her growing emptiness had been born out of guilt and regret. Tears erupted from her eyes, as she watched the rain pour down from the heavens.

She needed air. She ran to the front door, yanked it open, and stepped out onto the patio. She gasped for air. Within seconds, the rain drenched her clothes and skin, but it wasn't enough to wash away the emotional pain of having life ripped from her womb. She inhaled deep breaths, but still felt like she was suffocating. The tears continued to pour from her eyes like the rain that was drenching her body. She stepped inside and collapsed on the floor, sobbing.

"God, please forgive me," she choked out in a whisper. She had assumed this "treatment" would bring closure and resolution to her "illness." Instead, she had opened her heart's door to a new inhabitant—this time, an unwelcome one. Her heart throbbed as if it had been stabbed, and the wound had been left open to the elements. At the same time, her heart burned in her chest, and she felt like it might explode. The abortion was supposed to fix her mistake, not create a new, painful, and everlasting torment.

Chapter 1

Present, October 2009

The phone rang at approximately 1:00 a.m. Dr. Delaney Bartlett rolled over and answered her cell phone, "Hello?" The voice on the phone was Krissy from Labor and Delivery at St. Jo's Medical Center North in Guntersville, Alabama. Her deep, Southern draw made her words difficult to decipher.

"Dr. Bartlett, we need ya to come in now. A Hispanic gravida four para three just arrived. She looks like she's full term, and she's six centimeters dilated."

Delaney popped up out of bed and said, "I'll be right there." She brushed her teeth with lightning speed and threw on her shoes. Then, she grabbed her purse and raced out to her car.

She had a 15-minute drive to the hospital. Her heart pounded in her chest as she had gone from asleep to awake and driving in only a few minutes. In the dark, it was hard to see Lake Guntersville as she crossed over the bridge. She turned right at the bottom of the bridge and drove along the lakeside. Then, in the moonlight, as she glanced toward the lake, she could see the gentle, glistening ripples in the water. For a moment, she relaxed and noticed the beauty.

The Guntersville area, with its surrounding towns of Arab, Boaz, and Albertville, was heavily populated by Hispanic families, who worked in the poultry facilities. The Hispanic women rarely sought prenatal care for lack of insurance reasons. Instead, they would just show up in labor ready for delivery. The nurses called them "stop and drop" deliveries, because they occurred that way so often. The women would just "stop" in to the hospital and immediately "drop" or deliver a baby. Delaney had almost missed three of these deliveries in the last week. Upon hearing that the patient tonight was already six centimeters and having her fourth baby, Delaney knew she had better book it to the hospital if she wanted to make it in time for the delivery.

As she arrived to the floor, the nurses waved her into labor and delivery room three.

Once in the room, Krissy said, "The baby is crownin'." Krissy grabbed Delaney's gloves and held them out to her.

Delaney asked, "Does she speak English?"

Krissy replied, "No, not at all."

Delaney asked, "What is her name?"

Krissy answered, "Maria Alvarez."

Delaney barely had time to put her gloves on before she caught the baby. Soon after, the healthy baby boy was crying vigorously as Delaney clamped and cut the umbilical cord. Delaney looked up at Maria's abdomen and commented, "She still looks pregnant." Delaney examined the patient and said, "There's another baby, and it's transverse." She tried to manually rotate the baby, but she was unable to. Then, she said to Krissy, "Take her back to the OR and call anesthesia. We need to do a stat C-section."

Maria's husband spoke some English, so Delaney explained to him that there was a second baby that needed to be delivered by C-section. Maria's husband's eyes grew wide, and he explained the situation to Maria in Spanish. Maria's eyes grew wide, and her mouth dropped open. Then, she exclaimed something in Spanish. They both appeared to be trying to assimilate this shocking news. After a few moments of a Spanish-speaking exchange between Maria and her husband, the husband, still looking shocked, smiled at Delaney and commented in broken English, "We just thought baby was big!"

The second baby was a girl and was delivered by C-section in breech presentation. The surgery was uneventful. As shocking as this news was to the new parents, Delaney was not surprised. She was accustomed to these situations, and she was thankful that her training had equipped her for such acute challenges.

After the surgery, Delaney sat at the nurses' station, finishing her paperwork.

"Dr. Bartlett," said a woman's voice. Delaney looked up to see Krissy.

"Maria is askin' to see ya."

Delaney answered, "Okay, be right there." She finished her paperwork and then walked into the recovery room, where Maria was holding both babies, one in each arm.

Her husband smiled and spoke for her, saying, "We want to thank you for deliver babies and for help Maria."

Delaney smiled and replied, "You're welcome. I'm glad I could be part of it." She turned to walk away, and she heard Maria say something in Spanish to her husband.

"Excuse me, Doctor," her husband said.

"Yes?" replied Delaney, turning toward them.

"Could you hold babies and let us take picture?"

Delaney smiled but felt a hesitation rising in her stomach. She loved her job, but this part was always hard for her. She tried not to get too close to the babies she delivered. She felt undeserving of their love or of bonding with them in any way. Despite the familiar, uneasy feeling, she smiled and stepped forward reaching for both babies, one at a time.

"Of course, I would love that," she said. She held the babies for a few pictures and then gently handed them back to Maria.

Delaney knew in her heart and soul why she had chosen to become an obstetrician. It wasn't just because she loved babies or because it was her favorite rotation in medical school. In her heart, she needed to try to redeem herself, even just a little, for the poor decision she had made long ago. Her reason for studying and training for twelve years to have the ability to save the lives of babies wasn't so she could launch a career as a doctor. Her reason was deeply rooted in her soul. She had a debt to repay—except this debt was not a financial one that could be paid back. It was one she knew she could never fully repay. She hoped that, in time, bringing life into the world would somehow make up even just a little bit for what she owed to her own discounted child. She had carried the guilt and pain from that decision in her heart since the day it had happened. Although she was in the business of saving babies, she still had trouble feeling worthy of holding them. She felt shame. She wondered if she would ever be worthy of having her own child.

She had prayed about it many times, asking God to forgive her, but no matter how much she prayed, her feelings of guilt still did not lessen. But even more than the shame or guilt, it was the pain of the memory that drove her to strive for excellence with every patient and with every pregnancy for which she cared. She had chosen her purpose in life to be about bringing life safely into the world. She was protecting life. Although her work was a daily attempt to redeem herself, it still didn't relieve her pain for long.

Delaney yearned for a family of her own, but she couldn't see herself ever really deserving one. The feelings of guilt and shame came to surface any time she had thoughts of having a child. She tried to reason the idea of motherhood away and would tell herself she was too old anyway. She had passed her prime child-bearing years, and on top of that, she was doubtful that she'd meet the man of her dreams in small town United States. In her attempt to see a brighter side, she tried to focus on the positives. The fact that she didn't have her own family gave her the time and flexibility to be more present for her patients. Plus, she had a lot of downtime when she went home each evening. Despite her positive mental reinforcements, however, her heart still longed for a child. She prayed every day that someday, somehow, she would allow herself to feel worthy enough to have and love her own child and family.

Delaney's thoughts were interrupted, as she sat at the nurse's station.

Krissy sat down beside her, "So, Dr. Bartlett, how do ya like it here so far? You've been here for, what, maybe one month now?"

"Yes," Delaney answered, smiling. "I really like the town and the hospital. This town is just right for me right now."

Krissy asked, "Ya didn't bring any family with ya?"

Delaney answered, "No, I'm single. No kids." She hesitated after thinking of kids and then continued. "This place is just what I need right now."

Krissy smiled. Delaney really like Krissy. She wore her heart on her sleeve, and she radiated a genuine personality. In fact, most of the people in the town seemed very genuine. Delaney loved that about Guntersville. It was truly a place of Southern hospitality and comfort.

"Dr. Bartlett, I find it hard to believe you're not datin' anyone. Do ya have a boyfriend back in Kentucky?" Then, she added, "I hope ya don't mind me askin'."

Delaney exhaled and smiled. "No, it's fine. You can ask." She paused for a minute and then started again, "I was engaged to a guy, a doctor, for four years. It just didn't work out, and I needed a change. So moving here has actually been therapeutic for me."

Krissy looked sad, "I'm so sorry, Dr. Bartlett. That's a long time to be with someone. Is there any chance ya might get back together?"

"No," Delaney answered without hesitation. He's actually engaged to someone else. It didn't take him long to move on. In fact, he started moving on before he broke up with me, if you know what I mean."

Krissy put her hand over her mouth showing her shock. "I'm so sorry. What a jerk."

"I'm okay," replied Delaney. "It gets easier every day."

"How long ago did it happen, if ya don't mind me askin'?" Krissy asked.

Delaney smiled at Krissy's polite manner. "He broke up with me about six months ago, and he was engaged a week later."

"Oh my gosh!" Krissy exclaimed. "What a double jerk," she said, "if that's even a term. If it's not, it should be for guys like him." Then, she added with a jovial tone, "We need to fix ya up with a true, Southern gentleman."

Delaney smiled and shook her head. "Thanks, Krissy. You are very sweet, but I'm just fine. I really don't need a man in my life right now, either."

Krissy seemed dumbfounded. She just sat there shaking her head in disbelief. Then, she added, "Well, don't worry. Ya won't become the gossip of the town. People don't need to know your business. You're secret is safe with me."

Delaney chuckled and said, "It's no secret, but I would appreciate not being the talk of the town."

Krissy motioned her fingers across her lips as if to zip them closed. Then, she unzipped her lips and said, "You'll have to come to dinner one night at my house. Bryan and the kids would love to meet ya. Joey is eight and Vanessa is ten, and they would think it's cool to have a doctor come to dinner. Let me know when you're free."

Delaney replied, "I'd love that, as long as you don't try to fix me up with a Southern gentleman."

Krissy smiled as she got up and returned to Maria's bedside to assist her with the babies.

Delaney had come to Guntersville, Alabama, to join the obstetrics and gynecology practice of an old friend and colleague, Finn Donovan. They had done their residency training together back in Kentucky at the University of Louisville. Delaney had graduated from college, as planned, with a degree in chemical engineering; and then, she had decided to continue on to medical school and training to become a doctor.

This job with Finn was just what she needed to help her move past her ex-boyfriend. After sharing four years with her, Dr. Pierce Barretto announced he was not interested in getting married and then abruptly moved to New York to open a plastic surgery practice. Within one week of his move, he was engaged to a fellow plastic surgeon and much younger woman by the name of Alexis Devereaux. Delaney had been devastated. She knew that their relationship had endured some hardships, but she had no idea he had been cheating.

She was thirty-nine now, and she had been so sure that she and Pierce would marry. She felt like he had been her last chance at having children, since her fertility was waning at her older maternal age. After her initial heartache and period of distress, she had become weary of all the questions about Pierce and Alexis back home in Kentucky. Right after the break up, she would tear up when anyone asked her about Pierce and what had happened. But after a few weeks, the mention of his name just infuriated her. She realized she needed a fresh start away from the questions and memories, and this opportunity in Alabama had been the perfect chance to escape into small town oblivion.

Delaney finished her dictation and paperwork and started to head home. Before she could leave the parking lot, however, her phone cell rang. "Hello, this is Dr. Bartlett," she answered.

"Hey, Dr. Bartlett, this is Dr. Paine down in the ER. I have a patient here who has a torsed right ovary by CT scan and ultrasound."

Delaney replied, "Okay, I'm here in the hospital. I'll come down and see her now."

Dr. Paine replied, "Great, thanks."

Delaney was glad she hadn't gotten far on her journey home. An ovary twisted on itself, or torsed, meant there was no blood supply to that ovary. It was considered an emergency situation. If she didn't take the patient to surgery to "untwist" the ovary, it would have to be removed. She went to the ER and evaluated the patient. Afterward, she sat down at the physicians' desk to write preoperative orders and to make necessary phone calls.

"Hi there, Dr. Bartlett," said a friendly, male voice. Delaney turned to see a handsome, clean-cut man with brown hair and broad shoulders. His eyes were a striking sapphire blue, and he was smiling at her.

"Hi," Delaney said tentatively with a *Do I know you?* tone in her voice.

"I'm Doc Paine. We just spoke on the phone."

Delaney scrunched her nose and furrowed her eyebrows and asked, "Your last name is actually "Pain?"

He chuckled, "Yes, it's spelled P-a-i-n-e," he replied. "I'm a walking oxymoron, I know," he added, as if he were reading her thoughts about being a doctor with "pain" as his last name. He held out his hand to her and said, "I recognize you from the practice advertisement pictures. It's great to have you here."

Delaney reached for his hand and shook it. She replied, "It's so nice to meet you, Dr. Paine."

"It's Doc." He read her confused expression and commented, "Doc is my nickname. Everyone calls me that."

She smiled and said, "Okay, Doc. Call me Delaney."

He winked at her and then asked, "So are you taking this patient to surgery?"

She stared at him. His blue eyes were mesmerizing. She didn't think she had ever seen eyes that shade of blue, and she wondered if he might be wearing contacts.

She surveyed his face, as she answered him, "Yes, I'm calling the surgery manager now." His face had a genuine quality about it. She also couldn't help but notice his strong jaw line and full lips. She could see the hint of a dimple on his chin. He was attractive.

"Okay, great," he said. He then added, "I look forward to working with you."

She wouldn't mind working with him at all, she thought. A few seconds passed, and she realized she was staring at him. She glanced back at her paperwork and then back at him and replied, "Yes, I'm looking forward to working with you as well. Thanks for your help." She sat down as Doc walked off. She regrouped after being mesmerized by "Doc Sapphire" and called the surgery manager's pager number. She immediately got a call back.

"Hello," Delaney said.

"Hey, this is Ben Montgomery. Did you page me?" asked the voice on the line.

Delaney replied, "Yes, this is Dr. Bartlett with gynecology. I hope I'm not bothering you."

He didn't respond right away, and the silence felt awkward to Delaney. "What do you need?" he asked.

Delaney hesitated for a second. She hadn't expected him to seem aloof, especially in regard to a patient call. She said, "I need to take a patient to the OR for a diagnostic laparoscopy and possible right oophorectomy."

Ben replied, "Is this an emergency?"

Delaney could feel her blood pressure rising. She replied, "Of course, this is an emergency case. She is probably going to lose that ovary."

She heard a big exhale from him that sounded begrudging, and then, he said reluctantly, "All right, I'm on my way. I'll call the surgery team in. Give us thirty minutes, and we'll be ready to go."

Delaney hung up the phone and stared at it for a minute. He had been annoyed with her. She hadn't even met the man, and he had already spoken to her with disdain. She couldn't help but feel offended. What was his problem? Her case was emergent, this was her job, and if he didn't want to be called into surgery at night, he shouldn't have signed up for his job. As far as she was concerned, patient care came first, and if he had a problem with that, she would give him a piece of her mind. She sat back in her chair and crossed her arms. She pictured some short, half-bald guy with a potbelly, who was probably at home with his feet propped up on the coffee table, eating pizza and watching football. "Sorry to disturb you, Mr. Lazy," she muttered under her breath.

She arrived in the preoperative area to see her patient again and to check her labs and see if she had any last-minute questions. The anesthesiologist was preparing the patient for surgery. After Delaney spoke with the patient, she rounded the corner to see where in the heck Mr. Lazy was and why he wasn't there yet. As she turned the corner, she ran straight into a very large man.

"Oh sorry," she heard him say as he caught her and kept her from falling backward. His chest was so massive and hard that her petite 5'2" frame had ricocheted off him.

Delaney was dazed from the impact for a second. She finally regained her composure and then looked at him. She stood dumbfounded for a moment with her mouth open. The man was incredibly gorgeous. She couldn't help but gawk as she tried to take him in fully. He was tall and broad-shouldered and had massive arms and an obviously toned chest. His face held two deep-set dark brown eyes, full lips, and a sculpted jawline. His hair was short, wavy, and brown, and he actually had a small superman curl on his forehead.

She exhaled and thought, *Really, a Superman curl? Was this guy for real?* For a moment, they just stared at each other.

Finally, he grunted and asked, "Are you ready yet?" His less than charming attitude brought her back to reality.

She answered with irritation in her voice, "I'm sorry, do I know you?"

He replied with the same irritation in his voice, "Yeah, you just called me in for this surgery."

Delaney felt shocked. This was Ben Montgomery? He was not quite what she had pictured, not even close. Her thoughts raced as she tried to process that this handsome, well-built man was the arrogant jerk she had spoken with on the phone earlier. And he was still an arrogant jerk. She tried not to show her irritation with his attitude and decided to take the high road. She held out her hand to shake his and said, "I'm Delaney Bartlett. You must be …"

He seemed a little flustered, as he said, "Ben Montgomery." He didn't move to shake her hand at first, and she continued to hold it out to him. Finally, he stepped forward and took her hand.

Delaney felt a jolt of electricity in their touch. For just a moment, his eyes met hers. She studied him for that moment. In that brief exchange, she was certain that she had read an unmistakable sadness in those baby browns. That sadness disarmed her irritation just a little, and she exhaled and said, "It's nice to meet you."

He let go of her hand and muttered, "Yes, well, are you ready for me to take the patient back?"

She replied, "Ready when you are," giving him an uncertain smile.

But he didn't smile back. The man had an awesome exterior for sure, but underneath, he was grouchy and rude. She wasn't sure what his problem was. Maybe he was mad that she had torn him away from a football game, or maybe he was enjoying time with his wife, and he didn't like to be called in to the hospital at this hour. Although she had looked at his left hand, there was no wedding ring. *What a waste of a handsome man,* she thought. Delaney shook her head and dismissed any more thoughts of the aloof man, as she headed back to the OR for surgery.

Once the surgery was over, Delaney sat in the recovery room near the patient and wrote postoperative orders. She looked up at Ben, who was sitting at his desk working on some paperwork. She walked over to him and asked, "Do you know what room she's going to?"

He looked up and gave her a short reply, "No, they haven't assigned one yet."

She asked, "Well, can you call me when you know what room she's going to?"

He didn't look up this time from his paperwork and said, "I'll have her nurse call you." He didn't look at her at all, and he said nothing else.

She tried to shrug off his rudeness. "Thanks," she said and then walked off thinking, *He may be gorgeous, but he lacks some serious people skills.* With that thought, she headed home.

Chapter 2

Ben Montgomery leaned back in a kitchen chair. He glanced out the window of his lake house. Lake Guntersville looked especially calm and peaceful on this Saturday morning. The fog was thick and lingering low over the lake. The sun was rising, and he could see hues of pink and blue. The mixed hues gave the sky a light purple color. It was beautiful, though he wouldn't admit it. Nothing was really beautiful to him anymore. The November morning was unusually cold, signaling the approaching winter months in Alabama.

He arose and took his coffee out onto the front porch. He inhaled the crisp air and took a seat in one of the two Adirondack chairs on the porch. He sat quietly sipping his coffee, listening to the quiet sounds from the lake. The sadness he felt was still overwhelming at times. It had been eight years since the accident, but he was sure he would never stop feeling the pain. He missed them so much. They had been taken away so suddenly, without any warning.

Ben stood up, as if to distract himself from the painful memories. He walked back inside to make breakfast, but then decided against eating. He wasn't hungry. The lump in his throat made him feel nauseated. He knew he would never be free of the haunting memory.

He had been required to identify his wife and baby daughter after the car accident. There they lay, lifeless beside each other on separate stretchers. His wife, even lifeless and bloodied, had still been so beautiful. His baby daughter had only been two years old. The thought of her tiny body, broken and bloody, tore his insides out.

Tears filled his eyes and trickled down his cheeks onto the kitchen counter. He wiped the tears away with his hands. The raw visual of the two loves of his life hadn't faded, and he couldn't shake the memory no matter how hard he tried.

He had moved from their family home in San Diego, California, across the country to Guntersville to escape the memories. His friends and family back home were daily reminders of what he had lost. He couldn't stand for another person to look at him with such pity, though he understood that they just cared and didn't know what to say to him. Here in Guntersville, he had at least escaped the constant barrage of phone calls and cards and people feeling sorry for him. Although it was thoughtful, none of it would bring back Danna or baby Ella.

He just wanted them back. He wanted to hold his wife in his arms again, to love her, to hear her tell him to stop leaving his shoes where she would trip over them. He longed to hear her yell at him for anything, if he could just have her back. And Ella, that little girl had wrapped him around her precious, tiny pinky from the first time he had held her and looked into her sweet little eyes. She had said, "da-da," for the first time, and his heart had almost combusted with joy. He just wanted to hold the little bundle of her in his arms and kiss her sweet chubby cheeks. He wanted to feel her warm, tiny body snuggled into his chest, just one more time.

Ben put his face in his hands and sobbed. He prayed for strength, but he really just wanted God to take him home to heaven so he could be with them again. "Why did you leave me here?" He cried out. "I can't live like this. I can't bear this anymore. Why would you take them from me?"

He still felt angry with God. Some days, the pain of the memories was worse than other days, but today was just a hard day. It was the anniversary of their death. Danna and Ella had headed out on a morning just like this one, except it was foggy and cool from the marine layer coming off the ocean. They were just going to pick up a few groceries. They were supposed to be right back. A car had run a red light and T-boned Danna's car on the driver's side. Both of them had been killed instantly. Ben shuttered as he remembered the phone call from the police. He had been out on a plumbing job and had been called to come to the hospital.

A year later, when he was still drowning in grief, his mom had encouraged him to go back to school. Plumbing had been a decent occupation for him, but he needed something more to distract him from his pain. He agreed with his mom and decided to study nursing. He knew the difficulty of nursing would require a major commitment from him. He wouldn't have time to dwell on his pain. So he worked most days plumbing and then went to night school to get his nursing degree. Between the two ventures and exercising with a voracious appetite, he wore himself out, since sleep didn't come easily. The recurrent nightmares made him not want to sleep, but the worn-out shell of a man would eventually fall asleep from exhaustion.

Four years later, with his nursing degree in hand, he knew he had to move away. There was no way he could work in the same hospital where his wife and daughter had been pronounced dead. He wanted to run far, far away, as if to run from the memories. The job in Guntersville had been posted when he graduated. Guntersville would mean small-town medicine, but Ben liked the idea. He hoped a small town would give him the peace and quiet he longed for. So far, Guntersville had given him quiet for sure, but not peace. He wondered if he would ever have a sense of peace again.

His thoughts were interrupted with a text message from Krissy at work.

"Hey, Ben, Dr. Bartlett asked me for long Brown forceps yesterday during a C-section. Can you get those for us up in Labor and Delivery so we'll have them on hand for her?"

Ben texted, "Sure, I'll order them on Monday."

Ben's thoughts turned to Dr. Bartlett. Now, that woman was a piece of work. What was her first name, "Delaney?" She had just marched in like the new sheriff in town. What was she trying to prove? She bothered him, but he wasn't sure why. The few times he had interacted with her, he had felt irritation and impatience with her. He couldn't nail it down, but there was just something about her that frazzled him.

"Be nice," he said out loud to himself. He knew she was single, and there was a rumor about her big-time plastic surgeon ex-boyfriend running off with another woman. He felt a little bad for her.

Like him, she was also running away from bad memories. And, aside from her tough exterior, she seemed kindhearted, though he had only worked with her a few times. He exhaled a big sigh. She was also easy on the eyes.

Then, it hit him. For the first time since Danna, Ben realized he had found another woman attractive. Her long, wavy brown hair was always pulled up in a neat ponytail. Her petite build was slender and attractive. Her smile melted his inner core. Her green eyes had been piercing when he had first met her, as if they could see into his soul. No other woman except Danna had made his heart feel anything, until now.

Chapter 3

Delaney rolled over in her bed. The clock said 6:34 a.m. "Why can't I ever sleep in?" she groaned. This was her week off, and it was Saturday. She covered her head with the covers, hoping sleep would return to her eyes, but it was too late. Her mind was already jumping from one subject to another. "Pierce," she whispered. *Darn him.* Why did he always have to intrude her thoughts? "I'm not letting you destroy another single day for me, Pierce Barretto," she said out loud.

She threw back the covers. The house was chilly. She got out of bed and put on her robe and slippers. She ventured to the thermostat as she shivered. "Brrrr," she said. The thermostat read sixty-five. She clicked the heat on and set the thermostat to seventy. She walked through the living room to the kitchen and put on a fresh pot of coffee. The house was a new construction back in the Lake Guntersville Club. Most of the houses were on or near the lake. People that lived on the lake had individual docks for their boats. Delaney's house was built on a steep hill that backed up to a small pond just a short distance from the lake. It had been the only one available when she had been house hunting a few months earlier. It was a little big for one person, with its four bedrooms, but the back and side of the house had a wrap-around, partially screened-in porch. She loved the porch. She also enjoyed the secluded location of the house. It was quiet, and she could sit on her porch morning and night listening to the sounds of nature.

She poured a cup of coffee and ventured out to the screened-in porch. The November air was crisp and cool. She welcomed the fall weather and was thankful to live in a part of the country where she was able to experience all four seasons. She had been told that winters in Alabama were mild and that she might expect to see a few dustings of snow as winter approached. Delaney liked a few good snowfalls during the winter, so she would have to take what she could get here. She looked up at the sunrise and couldn't help but notice the pretty colors. She could see hues of pale pink and blue mixed together forming tones of light purple.

"Lavender sky," she said out loud. That's what her mom had called a light purple sunset one day. Delaney remembered being at her mom's bedside that day. Her mom had been really sick, suffering from the effects of the chemotherapy she was taking for ovarian cancer treatment. Delaney was only six years old then, but she had tried to remember every single memory of her mom.

Her mom had said, "A lavender sky is God's way of telling you that good things are coming."

Delaney smiled to herself, but then felt sadness. Nothing good had come for her mom. She had passed away only a few months later, right after Delaney's seventh birthday. She missed her parents. Her dad had never been the same after her mother's death. He had developed early Alzheimer's disease at the age of fifty and passed away within four years. Delaney recalled how his last few years were free of the painful memories of losing her mother, because he couldn't remember her. Although the disease was awful, she took some comfort in seeing that his grief had left him. During his last two years, he had forgotten who Delaney was. He had been gone for six years now. She missed both of her parents so much. Being an only child made her feel more alone. She really had no family left.

She stared at the lavender sky, as a tear trickled down her cheek. How had she gotten here? No parents, no husband, and no family. Maybe she was getting what she deserved. No matter how hard she tried, she couldn't stop punishing herself for her abortion. It had been twenty years, but she could not forget. Oh how she hated to allow that word to even enter her mind. But she had done it, and she understood why many other women had done it. She whispered, "Lord, let me change this path for at least one woman. Please use me to make a difference. I know you've forgiven me, but I struggle to forgive myself. Help me to do some good for another young, scared woman."

Delaney was glad to have her sad thoughts interrupted by a text from Krissy.

It read, "Hey, I just texted Ben. He's going to order those long Browns for you on Monday."

Delaney squealed, "Oh good." She texted back, "Thank you," as she rolled her eyes at herself for getting so excited over a surgical instrument.

Her thoughts turned to Ben. This man had caught her attention. Why was he so grumpy and rude? A man who looked as good as he did shouldn't be allowed to be irritable. Come to think of it, she hadn't seen him smile even once. There had to be a story there, but she couldn't imagine what could possibly make him want to be so sour. She hadn't detected a Southern accent and wondered if he was a transplant to the area. She didn't know why, but she found herself wanting to know more about him. He was attractive, no doubt. She had ricocheted off his six-foot Superman build, and then, she'd embarrassed herself by gawking at him with her mouth hanging wide open. That was not one of her better moments, she would admit. Aside from his gorgeous looks, however, she had remembered his eyes. There was something mysterious in his eyes, a sadness and longing that had reached her heart. She knew there was more to him, and she wanted to know what it was.

Chapter 4

On Monday, Delaney stopped by the hospital cafeteria for a café mocha on her way to her office. She had finished hospital rounds and was feeling hungry. While she was there, she decided to grab a dozen strawberry muffins to take to her office staff. After making her purchase, she picked up her mocha and the bag of muffins and spun around toward the exit. As she turned, she saw Ben coming in. She decided to be cheerful to see if she could get a smile out of him.

"Good morning," she said with a chipper voice and a big smile.

Ben looked at her as he passed by, but then glanced away and muttered, "Morning."

Delaney proceeded to her office and dropped the muffins off in the kitchen. She had Ben on her mind. Why couldn't the guy be friendly, at least? Did he have a problem with everyone or just her? What a waste of good looks!

Delaney's train of thought was interrupted. Her medical assistant, Candace, peeked into the kitchen smiling and said a melodic, "Hello-oh!" Delaney wasn't sure where Candace got her cheerfulness, but she wanted to squeeze some of it out of her and pour it onto Ben.

"Hi," Delaney replied. "I brought some yummy, strawberry muffins over from the cafeteria."

Candace seemed overly happy to be getting muffins, "Thank ya so much. How thoughtful!" Then, she added, "Those are Dr. Donovan's favorites, so grab one while ya can!"

Delaney headed to her office. She set her purse and mocha down and took off her coat. She hung it on the wall hook and then put on her white coat. She sat down and took a healthy swig of her mocha.

"Good morning, Delaney. Do you have a minute?" asked Finn as he plopped down in one of the chairs across from Delaney's desk.

"Hey, sure," she answered. "How are you today?"

He took a drink of his coffee and replied, "Good. I just finished a scope for an ectopic pregnancy. The tube was ruptured."

Delaney asked, "Did your patient do okay?"

He answered, "Yeah, she did fine." Finn laid back in his seat running his fingers over his dark brown goatee and asked, "So, how are you liking it here so far? It's been a little over two months. Are you feeling good about everything and everyone?"

Delaney smiled, "Yeah, I'm impressed with the hospital and everyone here. I've had a warm welcome by everyone. Well, almost everyone."

He furrowed his brow, "Have you had problems with someone here?"

She replied, "Not here, but over at the hospital."

He sat up and leaned forward, "What's going on?"

Delaney replied, "Oh, it's not a patient care or surgery issue. It's just that Ben Montgomery guy. He is so rude to me."

Finn was silent and looked as if he was carefully planning his words.

"What?" She asked.

"Well," said Finn. "He's not a troublemaker, and he is usually somewhat cordial. Sounds like he's singled you out for the rudeness, though. My wife and I have had him over for dinner a few times. He's not usually rude. I'm not sure what the deal is there."

Delaney shook her head and then asked, "What's his story anyway?"

Finn got up and closed the door. He sat back down.

"He's not a convicted felon or anything, is he?" Delaney chuckled.

"No," said Finn. "I wish his story was different than it is, though."

She furrowed her eyebrows and said, "That bad, huh?"

Finn took a deep breath and then said, "Ben moved here from California after his wife and two-year-old daughter were tragically

34

killed in a car accident. It happened about eight years ago. Not many people know his story, and he wants to keep it that way. He has not been able to move past his grief and understandably so."

Delaney gasped and shook her head. She felt her heart sink, and she could only imagine the pain Ben must be going through. She remembered how sad his eyes were when she had first met him. Now, it made sense. He was sad beyond words. She suddenly felt ashamed of the thoughts she'd had about him.

"I feel so bad for calling him rude," she said to Finn.

"Don't feel bad," he said. "Ben comes off aloof, and you didn't know his story until now."

She sighed, "Well, thanks for letting me know. I have a better understanding now."

Finn stood up and said, "Well, the patients are waiting."

She rolled her eyes, "So many on the schedule today. You had better get a strawberry muffin. I brought them in this morning."

Finn replied, "Oh, I know. I've already had three!"

Delaney giggled as Finn left. She turned her attention to the stack of charts on her desk. The first patient on her list was Savannah Carter. She thumbed through the charts until she came across Savannah's chart. Just a few days prior, she had seen this young woman in her office for the first time. Savannah was a twenty-one-year-old new pregnant patient. Delaney had done an ultrasound showing her the eighteen-week baby in utero. The baby was kicking and waving and moving all over the place, but Savannah wouldn't look at the baby. Instead, she had turned her head away. This had bothered Delaney, as she recalled their troublesome conversation.

"Is everything okay?" Delaney had asked Savannah.

Savannah replied, "I just have a lot of stressors right now. This isn't a good time to be pregnant."

Delaney had tried to lighten the situation and said, "It never is a good time, is it? Did you know that most pregnancies are not planned?"

Savannah didn't change her expression. She looked down at the floor and would barely make eye contact with Delaney. She seemed sad and hopeless. After the ultrasound, Delaney obtained more of

Savannah's medical history. Savannah told her this was her third pregnancy and that she already had two boys, ages two and one. She volunteered to Delaney that her mom had custody of her two-year-old and said that it was "because I just can't take care of two kids right now."

Delaney asked, "Is the father of the baby involved?"

Savannah replied, "Yeah," but that's all she offered. Savannah didn't want to talk about it anymore. Delaney reluctantly stopped asking questions. She ordered her prenatal labs that day, prior to Savannah leaving her office, and then scheduled her follow-up visit in four weeks.

Delaney closed the chart and felt anxiety while remembering Savannah's reaction to her pregnancy. Savannah seemed to be hopeless, and that was not a good place to be.

Chapter 5

Delaney stepped into exam room one. "Good morning, Savannah. How are you today?" She asked smiling. Savannah was sitting on the exam room table. She was wearing a navy sweatshirt, faded jeans, and old tennis shoes. Her blonde hair was stringy, and she looked disheveled.

Savannah looked up for a minute without smiling and replied, "Hi, I'm fine, but I guess I'm a little worried why you called me in here. It's only been a few days since I had an appointment." She wouldn't hold eye contact with Delaney and seemed to be shy or scared. Delaney sat down on the rolling stool and wheeled closer to Savannah.

"Savannah," Delaney started, "your platelet count is low." She went on to explain, "This may just be a pregnancy-related thing, or it may be a more serious issue. Platelets help your blood clot. If they get too low, you can have problems with bleeding, even hemorrhage."

Savannah was quiet for a minute and then said, "I think I had this problem in my other two pregnancies."

Delaney was hopeful this was true because then the diagnosis of gestational thrombocytopenia would be a more favorable one. "Well, I'd like to request your records from your previous deliveries, and I'll need your consent to get your records," Delaney said. She went on to say, "I wanted to bring you in here to discuss this with you face-to-face in case you had any questions."

Savannah was silent for several seconds. Finally, she looked up at Delaney with a stoic expression and said, "Dr. Bartlett, I can't keep this pregnancy."

Delaney's heart skipped a beat, and she took a deep breath. She wanted to understand Savannah correctly and asked, "What do you mean?"

Savannah looked away and said, "I need to have an abortion."

Delaney felt panic-stricken as she struggled to bear the weight of what Savannah had just said. She prayed silently, *Lord, tell me what to say. Tell me what to do*

Delaney was silent for a few seconds and then scooted her chair closer to Savannah. She looked into Savannah's eyes and asked, "Why do you feel this way?"

Tears collected in Savannah's eyes, as she tried to remain strong. Savannah continued to look at the floor and said, "Dr. Bartlett, I can't take care of another child. My mom has custody of my first child. My boyfriend and I can barely take care of my son who lives with us. I just got out of jail for drivin' without a driver's license, because I couldn't pay the court fine, and I still owe money to the court. I can't work and take care of my son. My boyfriend doesn't stay around much and hardly helps me with bills. I just can't take care of another kid." Savannah finally looked up hesitantly at Delaney, as if she was expecting to see judgment in Delaney's eyes. A tear rolled onto her chin, and she brushed it away with the back of her hand.

Delaney scooted back and grabbed the box of Kleenex off the counter. She stood and handed it to Savannah. After Savannah had wiped her face and regrouped, Delaney took Savannah in her arms and embraced her. Delaney knew that sometimes, words just weren't enough. She let go of Savannah after a few seconds and sat back down on her stool.

She asked Savannah, "Have you thought about adopting your baby out to a couple who can't have children?"

Savannah replied, "I've thought about it, but it scares me."

Delaney asked, "Why does it scare you?"

Savannah replied, "What if I can't find adoptive parents I like? How will I know if they will really love this baby? What if I adopt to the wrong couple, and they end up being bad parents?"

Delaney sat quietly. She was familiar with the emotions Savannah was expressing. Savannah was scared to death. Savannah had reasoned that instead of making more mistakes with this pregnancy, she would just end it. Delaney understood exactly how Savannah felt, because she had walked in her shoes.

Savannah looked up from the floor and looked at Delaney. Delaney had tears running down her cheeks too. The gravity of Savannah's situation and hopelessness had brought back Delaney's own feelings from years ago.

"Why are you crying, Dr. Bartlett?" Savannah asked and added, "I'm sorry if I made you sad."

Delaney tried to force a small smile. "Savannah," she started, "don't choose abortion. As much as you may feel like it's your only choice right now, it's not. And I promise you, it's one that you will regret for the rest of your life." Delaney paused, and in that moment, an understanding passed between the women.

"Well, I don't know how to do this adoption thing," Savannah said.

Delaney took a deep breath and said, "I will help you. Let's start by having our social worker sit with you and explain everything to you." She paused and then said, "Savannah, promise me you won't have an abortion."

Savannah seemed to be searching for an answer and then replied, "I can't promise."

Delaney felt the little life slipping away and began to feel a sense of urgency. "Okay, how about this?" Delaney went on, "You promise to adopt out your baby rather than abort. If you can't find parents for your baby, parents that will give you peace of mind, I will adopt your baby. It can be an open adoption, and you can come visit her anytime you want. Even if you change your mind and want to keep your baby, I'll be okay with that."

Savannah's eyes grew wide as she asked, "You would do that?"

Delaney replied without hesitation, "Absolutely. Look at me. I'm not married, I'm almost forty, and I probably won't be able to have kids." She smiled at Savannah, and for the first time ever, Savannah smiled back at her.

Delaney drove home after office that day. She thought that her discussion with Savannah would give her peace. Instead, Delaney felt uneasy. She felt excitement and fear rolled into one big ball in her stomach. The conversation with Savannah had been unexpected. Delaney thought again about the implications of what she had suggested to Savannah. The words had just poured off her lips not requiring any thought, as if she hadn't been the one to say them. What had she agreed to? In one conversation, she had basically agreed to adopt a newborn. Had she forgotten she would be an almost forty-year-old single mom with a busy, full-time OB/GYN practice? No, somehow none of those factors had been part of her reasoning that day. In fact, Delaney wondered if this is what happened to Moses when God said to him, "I will help you speak and will teach you what to say" (Exodus 4:12). Delaney looked to the sky and said, "Lord, I don't know where my words came from today. Was that the solution I was supposed to give to Savannah? I have to believe those were the words You wanted me to speak."

She felt anxious. She knew Savannah didn't have the necessary resources to raise another child; but geez, she hadn't even thought about what it meant to raise a child herself, alone, without a husband and father for the baby, and with her crazy schedule.

"Well, I'll just have to get a nanny," she said. No, she didn't want someone else raising her child. But how was she supposed to work and be a mom? How was she going to cover call and sleep with a newborn in the house? Delaney's thoughts were jumbled, and she began talking to herself out loud. Then, she quieted and realized that regardless of how it would play out, she knew she would do anything to spare the life of this baby.

Then, she thought, *Surely, Savannah will change her mind once she holds that baby in her arms. I know I would.* Delaney finally relaxed, as she realized that God had planned this just right. Maybe the words He had given her today with Savannah were the words she needed to speak life for this unborn baby.

"I'm just going to trust you on this one, Lord," Delaney said, as she pulled into her driveway.

Chapter 6

A few weeks later, Delaney approached Krissy's front door and pushed the doorbell. She heard the loud singsong chime of the doorbell and waited for a few seconds.

"Hey, Dr. B, welcome. Come on in," exclaimed Krissy, smiling as she opened the door and gently pulled Delaney in by her arm.

"Thank you for having me over," replied Delaney, as she stepped inside. Delaney handed Krissy a bottle of red wine.

"Thank you, but ya didn't have to bring anything," she said. Then, she added, "Here, give me your coat, and I'll hang it up."

Delaney peeled off her coat and gloves and handed them to Krissy. "Thanks," she said.

"Come on into the living room and have a seat. Bryan is in there. Dinner is almost ready. Would ya like a glass of wine?" asked Krissy.

"Yes, please, that would be great. I'm not on call tonight. Maybe a glass of wine will warm me up a bit. I didn't know it got this cold in Alabama in December," Delaney said.

Bryan was seated in the living room and arose from his reclining chair when Delaney entered the room. He smiled and held out his hand to her, "Welcome to our home. I'm Bryan, Krissy's better half." Krissy snickered at him and shook her head.

"Nice to meet you, and thanks for having me over. Dinner smells wonderful," said Delaney as she shook his hand.

"Have a seat over here by the fire," he said and motioned to the couch.

Krissy disappeared into the kitchen after hanging up Delaney's coat. She reappeared with three glasses of wine on a carrying tray and handed one to Delaney and one to Bryan. Krissy sat down in the recliner next to Bryan's. She took a sip of her wine and exclaimed, "Mmmm, this is delicious. Thank you for bringin' it."

Delaney replied, "I'm glad you like it. It's one of my favorites."

"So what have ya been up to this weekend?" Krissy asked.

"Oh, just usual home stuff. I've been cleaning and doing laundry, and I finally put my Christmas tree up," Delaney answered. She hadn't felt like putting up a tree this year, because she didn't feel like she had much to celebrate. Christmas had been her mom's favorite time of year, although the act of simply putting up the tree made her feel a little closer to her mom.

"Girl, I've had my tree up since November first. We love Christmas in this house," Krissy replied with a chuckle.

"What do ya mean 'we'?" asked Bryan, giving his wife a cute, flirtatious look.

"Darlin', do ya want to sleep on the couch tonight?" she teased him back.

"Never in a million years would I want to be separated from my beautiful wife," he replied. Then, he looked at Delaney raising his glass in the air and said, "We love Christmas in this house, and I do emphasize 'we'." Then, he reached over and held Krissy's hand. The two of them exchanged an endearing look.

This display of affection warmed Delaney's heart. She missed having a man in her life. She missed the companionship and the fun, playful banter. Krissy and Bryan had a magical relationship. She could see the love between them. As happy as she was to see their love for each other, it also made her heart ache. But it wasn't aching for Pierce. She was over him. Any man who could cheat wasn't worth another wasted ounce of energy. She let out a big exhale. She longed for that someone special to hold her hand, to hold her, and to love her. She wanted to share her life with someone.

Her wishful thoughts were interrupted as the doorbell rang. Delaney felt confused as she watched Krissy get up to go to the door. She wasn't expecting anyone else to be there. Who could it be?

"Ben, hi, come on in," Krissy said.

"Hey, Ben," Bryan said as he stood and walked over to Ben to shake his hand.

Delaney spun around on the couch to face the front door. Sure enough, there was Ben Montgomery. Her mouth gaped open in surprise. Ben stared back at her with just as much surprise in his expression.

"Hello, Dr. Bartlett," he said with some hesitation.

Delaney choked out, "Hi, Ben."

Krissy had obviously decided not to make her guest list public. Krissy took Ben's coat as he handed her a bottle of red wine. "Will ya look at that," Krissy said. "Ya both brought the same wine tonight. How amazin' is that?"

Ben looked good. Delaney's eyes were glued to him. He was wearing faded jeans and a black, tight, long-sleeved T-shirt and black boots. She could see the outline of his deltoid and pectoral muscles through his shirt. Why did he have to look so darn good? Delaney looked away as she felt her face flush, and she moved away from the fireplace. After a moment, she looked over at Ben and asked, "Have you been to Paso Robles?" The merlot she had brought was from her wine club in Paso Robles, California. She had been wine tasting there with Pierce and had fallen in love with the wine country there.

He replied, "I'm from San Diego. I've been to the wine country in Central California many times. I love the Villa Terre merlot. It's the best." Ben stared at her for a moment. She looked fine. The woman could wear some jeans and boots. Her hair was down and falling in soft curls around her face and shoulders. He had never seen her out of a ponytail. It had to be a sin for a woman to look that good. His brain snapped back to reality. What was she doing here anyway? He paused for a moment as he realized that Krissy was probably trying to set him up with her. "Nice try," he muttered under his breath, shaking his head, thinking that there was no way that he and "Doc Sheriff" were compatible.

"Oh well, I agree. What a coincidence that we have the same favorite wine," Delaney replied, as she gave Krissy a confused stare. She couldn't believe Krissy had invited Ben.

Krissy held up her hands in a surrender mode to Delaney and Ben and said, "Listen, y'all, before ya start wondering why I didn't tell y'all who would be here, just realize this is only an early Christmas dinner with friends. Bryan and I wanted to invite y'all both over because we enjoy makin' holiday dinners together for our friends, and we didn't want either of ya to be alone."

Ben felt relieved that Krissy had said something. He didn't want Delaney thinking he had arranged this little rendezvous.

Delaney relaxed as she was able to dismiss the same thoughts.

"Well, if dinner's ready, I'm ready for some good down home cooking," Ben said.

Bryan motioned toward the table, "Then, y'all head on into the dinin' room and get started."

Delaney pulled Krissy aside as Ben and Bryan disappeared into the dining room. "You didn't plan this dinner as a date for me and Ben, did you?"

Krissy smiled and said, "No, but that would have been a good idea. I think you two would be good for each other. Ya know his story, right?"

Delaney furrowed her brow, "Yes, Krissy. I know some of it, but I'm not looking to get fixed up with anyone, especially not him. He has been really hard to work with, and he's grumpy."

Krissy wrinkled her forehead as if she was confused, "What? Are ya kiddin'? He's the nicest guy, and he's so easy to work with. Plus, he's so easy on the eyes."

"Not from where I'm standing," Delaney said. "He's been rude to me, and I'm not interested in having to decipher his moods no matter how good he looks."

"Well, tonight, just enjoy dinner with friends, okay? 'Tis the season, right?" Krissy asked as she smiled and nudged her with her elbow.

"Okay, sure. I can do that. I am actually excited about a Southern home-cooked meal," Delaney replied. "I don't cook much, because it's just me. I'm looking forward to this meal. It smells wonderful."

Bryan and Ben were talking football as the two ladies entered the dining room. The two kids were already seated, so the only open seat for Delaney was across from Ben. Bryan introduced the kids to Delaney, and then, Delaney took her seat. Krissy brought the food in and set it in the middle of the table. Delaney had expected turkey and all the fixin's; but instead, the meal included Southern fried chicken, mashed potatoes, green beans, macaroni and cheese, and rolls.

The dinner chatter was relatively quiet. The kids each told what grade they were in and what things they were enjoying this school year. Eight-year-old Joey shared his Christmas list of desired toys for Christmas, while his twelve-year-old sister, Lizzie, rolled her eyes. Bryan and Ben discussed football a little more, while Delaney and Krissy talked about shopping and Christmas decorations.

Delaney had to admit that aside from having to sit directly across from Ben, which was nice but made her uncomfortable, the evening was nice. It felt good to be with a family and to feel like part of a family. She had felt alone for so many years, and although she had been with Pierce's family on occasion, she didn't get the same warm, fuzzy feeling from them.

Krissy disappeared into the kitchen temporarily and then returned to the dining room with a pie in each hand. She placed the two pies on the table, along with plates. "Dig in. Here is apple and pumpkin pie," she said, as she pointed at each pie.

Delaney and Ben both reached for the pumpkin pie at the same time. Their hands touched sending sparks of electricity up Delaney's arm. Ben felt it too. For a moment, they both pulled away their hands as if they'd been shocked and stared at each other.

"Ladies first. Please go ahead," Ben said. Ben had softened some throughout the evening, and the two of them had exchanged several awkward moments of eye contact. He hadn't smiled, but he had seemed to warm up to her a little.

Delaney reached for a piece of pie and said, "Thank you." An awkward silence followed until Krissy entered the room with a pot of coffee.

"Who wants coffee?" she asked. Bryan held up his mug.

"Over here, sweet mama," he said.

"Mom, can I have milk and a piece of apple pie?" asked Joey.

"I'll get the pie for him," said Ben, who was sitting next to him.

Delaney watched Ben serve a piece of pie to Joey. He was teasing Joey by giving him a thin slice of pie. Joey looked up at Ben unamused, until he realized Ben was teasing him. Ben half smiled in that moment and then served Joey a much bigger slice of pie. Joey's eyes widened, and his smile almost went eyebrow to eyebrow when he saw the size of the second slice. This was entertaining for Delaney. She hadn't seen any of Ben's personality except for his disdain for her. So, he could actually kid around. That was new. Maybe there actually was a soft heart under that grumpy exterior.

"Krissy, thank you so much for a delicious dinner, but I'm going to get going," said Ben.

"I should get going too. That was the best dinner I've had in a long time. I think I'll sleep well tonight. Thank you," Delaney said.

Ben left after a few goodbyes, and then, Delaney made sure to wait a few minutes so she wouldn't have to walk out with Ben.

"You're comin' to Winter Fest next weekend, right?" Bryan asked.

"I don't know what that is," replied Delaney.

"It's Guntersville's best festival of the year. There will be Christmas cheer, shoppin', and good food. Just come out and enjoy it. It's right down on the lake," said Bryan.

"Okay, I will if I'm not on call," she said. As she put her coat on to leave, Krissy handed her some leftovers.

"Here, take this home and eat it tomorrow. I was going to give Ben some leftovers, but he hightailed it out of here," said Krissy.

"His loss, my gain," replied Delaney, smiling. "I really had a great time. Thank you for including me. Have a good night."

Chapter 7

As Bryan had mentioned, the Guntersville Annual Winter Fest was the second Saturday in December. People from the surrounding towns turned out for this festive winter celebration at the lake every year. Everyone at the office was going, and Delaney was in the mood for some Christmas cheer, so she decided to venture out and check it out. Finn was on call tonight, so Delaney wouldn't have to worry about parking in a particular place so she could make a run for the hospital if a patient presented in labor.

The weather was a perfect fifty degrees, and the wind off the lake was minimal. Delaney finished a light, 15-minute yoga stretch and decided to leave on her snug yoga tank top and boy shorts. She figured layering would be the way to go tonight so she wouldn't have to wear a heavy coat. She walked into her closet and pulled on a long-sleeved shirt and then a thick, cotton black sweater along with dark, bootleg jeans. She slid her black walking boots on for comfort. Since the weather was cool, she decided to leave her hair down to add a little warmth. She picked out a scarf and gloves to bring with her as she knew the evening hours would bring cooler temperatures.

Delaney arrived at the festival at four o'clock and parked at the Guntersville Chamber of Commerce. It was one of the designated downtown parking lots for the evening. The crowd was just starting to build, as she arrived. All along the lake, several vendors had set up their tents. They were all decorated with red, white, and green twinkle lights. People and families were scattered up and down the lake along the tents. *Jingle Bell Rock* was blaring from a DJ station set up at one end. Just a short distance from the tents down by the lake was a bonfire. It was fenced off all around to keep the children a safe distance away. Several people were gathered around it for warmth.

Delaney walked along the lake and stopped in to shop at the various peddler tents. She purchased pottery, candles, dish towels, ornaments, and earrings. After an hour of shopping, her stomach was growling, and she headed toward the food vendors.

"Hey, Dr. B!" She heard someone yell from behind. Delaney turned toward the voice and saw Krissy walking up with Bryan and the kids.

"Hey, Krissy!" she replied.

"Are ya having a good time?" Krissy asked.

Delaney held up her bags and said, "Too good. I'm spending too much money."

"We're goin' to get a bite to eat. Want to come along?" asked Bryan.

Delaney smiled and said, "You read my mind. I'm starving!"

After they ate, Delaney excused herself to go wander a little more through the remaining peddler tents.

"Delaney!" She heard a voice from behind. She turned around and saw a smiling, handsome Doc Paine headed toward her. He was wearing a blue wool sweater and dark blue jeans. The blue in his sweater added a sparkle to his sapphire blue eyes.

"Hi, Doc," she replied with a big smile.

"So, how do you like the festival?" he asked.

Delaney laughed and held up her bags and replied, "A little too much."

"Have you eaten yet?" he asked.

"I ate dinner with Krissy and her husband, but I was just thinking of having a funnel cake," she replied.

Doc smiled, "Want to split one?"

Delaney smiled back, "That sounds great!"

Doc motioned to a picnic table and said, "Have a seat here, and I'll go get the funnel cake and two coffees."

Delaney nodded and took a seat. What a nice coincidence it was to run into Doc Sapphire. He was the kind of gentleman Delaney could get used to. She appreciated his kind demeanor and chivalrous nature. She felt good about hanging out with him for a little while tonight to get to know him better.

Doc returned with the cake and coffees and set them down on the table. He took a seat beside her. As they split the funnel cake, Doc asked, "So what do you think of our quaint little town?"

Delaney smiled and answered, "What's not to like?"

He scooted a little closer to her so he wouldn't have to yell over the crowd, "I hope you don't get your itch for the big city too soon and leave us. A lot of people, especially the young, single people, don't stay because they figure out Guntersville is not enough for them."

Delaney looked at him inquisitively, "What keeps you here? You're young and nice-looking. Why haven't you left yet?"

As he started to answer her, she heard a woman call for him, "Doc!" They both looked over and Delaney saw an attractive woman walking toward them and waving. Delaney recognized her as a nurse at the hospital.

"Hey, babe, I thought you were going to be a little later," Doc said to the approaching woman.

The woman walked up, and Doc put his arm around her. She answered, "There was low census at the hospital, so they let me go early."

"That's great," he said, as he kissed her cheek. He turned to look at Delaney and said, "Delaney, this is Millie, my fiancé. She works as a floor nurse on the fifth floor. Millie, this is Delaney, the new OB doc in town."

The two women shook hands and smiled at each other. Millie said, "I heard you were coming. It's so good to have you here. You'll have to come to dinner with us soon."

Delaney now understood why Doc stayed in this small town. Millie was the future Mrs. Doc Sapphire. She should have known he'd have someone. She liked Millie, though. She seemed sweet and genuine, and she and Doc also made a cute couple. Delaney had expected the scenario with herself and Doc to turn out differently, but it was okay. She found him attractive and charming, but there really had been no sparks.

"I would love that," Delaney replied to Millie.

After a few minutes of conversation, Delaney said, "Thanks for the cake and coffee, Doc. I'm getting cold, so I think I'll head home." Delaney excused herself after shaking hands with Millie again and waving at Doc. She walked toward her car and noticed how the moonlight was reflecting off the water. *How pretty and serene,* she thought.

When she reached her car, she decided she could use a slow, peaceful walk under the moonlight. She threw her bags and purse inside her car and then locked the car. She put on her gloves and scarf, since the temperature had dropped quite a bit. She put her keys in her pocket and walked further down the lake away from the crowds. The night was perfect for walking, and she felt the need to take a slow pace near the lake to relax and unwind.

When she approached an area of the lake that appeared to have a beachfront to it, she walked down to the edge of the water and looked out over the lake. She shivered, as she felt the breeze come off the surface of the water. The waves were picking up as the wind was becoming gusty. Despite the waves, the moonlight cast a ray of light that looked like it split the water right down the middle. It was beautiful. As she stared further out onto the lake, she thought she could see a small fishing boat. *Why in the heck would someone be out fishing at this hour?* she thought.

She leaned a little further out thinking she might be able to see better. Her weight shifted forward as she leaned out more, and she stepped forward so she wouldn't fall. Only, her foot could not find any part of the bank, and instead, it slid into the water. What she thought had been a shallow beach area wasn't. As her foot slid into the water, she lost her balance and fell in. She let out a yelp as she fell in, but then, she was completely submerged. Her body felt pain as the jolt of icy cold water shot through and pierced her bones.

As she came up to the surface for air, she took a deep breath and looked around trying to get her bearings. The moon now had cloud cover and was not showing its light. She couldn't see anything. Delaney reached for the bank, but she couldn't hold on. It was wet, slippery, muddy, and cold. She started yelling for help, but knew no one was anywhere near this area of the lake right now.

Lord, help me, she prayed while she frantically tried to hang onto the bank. It was of no use. She continued treading water and tried swimming to another part of the bank, but she didn't get far. It was too dark, she couldn't see anything, and she was getting tired. Her joints were becoming rigid from the cold. She felt overwhelming fear, but she kept struggling and then floating and then trying to find a place to get up on the bank. She wasn't sure how much longer she had before hypothermia would set in, but fatigue was taking over, and she tried to concentrate on staying afloat. As she worked to keep her head above the surface, uncontrollable shivering began. Delaney started to lose hope.

"Hey," she heard a voice from a few feet away. Delaney was sure she was imagining the voice, but it didn't matter anyway. She was too weak to respond. In the next moment, a strong hand reached down and grabbed her arm and then her other arm. She was lifted almost effortlessly into a small boat. She was still shivering and felt like she had no control over her frozen limbs. As she looked up to see what stranger had come to her rescue, the moon came out from behind the clouds. She blinked twice as to be sure her vision was clear. Ben Montgomery was kneeling over her.

"Don't you think it's a little cold and dark for a swim?" He asked jokingly trying to lessen her fear and the acuity of the situation.

She couldn't speak or intentionally move. She tried to focus on Ben again. As she did, she saw something she had never seen before. He smiled at her, and for an instant, she felt a surge of warmth come over her. She had never been happier to see anyone in her life.

"Thank you," she could barely choke out with tears forming in her eyes.

Ben worked quickly to strip Delaney down to her underclothes. "I'm sorry"—he said—"but I've got to get you out of these cold, wet clothes now."

Delaney understood and knew he was right. Thankfully, she was glad she had kept her yoga underclothes on. He took his hat off and put it on her head and then took his coat off and wrapped her up in it. As she lay in the boat, he tried to cover her with his body to warm her. He reached up and started the motor to the boat and then steered it while lying over her. He could feel her small frame shaking.

"Just hang on, Delaney. You're going to be fine," he said. Hearing him call her by her first name gave her a good feeling. She couldn't understand it, but it made him feel like home to her. It was personal and gave her comfort. Although he had spoken his words of assurance with confidence, in the moonlight, she could see that he was terrified.

As they approached his boat dock, he sat up and pulled her up next to him. He placed her head under his chin against his chest to keep her head covered as much as possible. When they reached the dock, he jumped out and secured the boat. He jumped back in the boat and lifted her and carried her into his house.

He took her to the bathroom and ran a warm bath for her. After pulling his coat and hat off her, he laid her down in the warm bath in her yoga tank and boy shorts. She was too weak to move on her own, and she was still shaking. He covered her with a towel so she wouldn't feel so exposed. He held onto her as he slowly warmed the water little by little. Eventually, her shaking lessened and color returned to her cheeks and lips. She was completely worn out from her struggle with the cold lake.

After the bath had warmed Delaney, Ben picked her up out of the tub and dried her off with a towel. She was unsteady on her feet, as she was still having episodes of the shakes keeping her off balance.

Ben looked at her, "Do you think you can manage to get out of those clothes and put on these clothes? I can help you if you can't."

He held out a men's sweatshirt, flannel pants, and thick socks, which she assumed were his. Delaney felt weak, but she wasn't about to give up anymore of her dignity. He had already stripped her down to her yoga apparel. She might as well have been in a bathing suit. Thankfully, it had been dark outside.

She nodded at him and said, "I'm sure I can manage."

He led her into his bedroom and sat her on the bed. "I'll just be right outside the door," he said as he turned to leave.

"No," Delaney said with as much force as she could muster. Then, her voice softened as she added, "Please, don't leave me."

Ben stared at the small-framed beauty and said, "Okay, I'll stand here with my back to you. I won't leave you alone. You can hang onto me for balance."

Delaney seemed satisfied with that. As he turned around, Delaney stopped him. She motioned to her back and weakly asked "Can you unsnap this please?" Her yoga tank had a clasp at the back of the neck just above a keyhole cutout. Her fingers were still too cold to perform such a tactical task.

He took a deep breath, as he realized this intimate task would be difficult for him. He hadn't been this close to a woman since Danna. He took another deep breath and then reached behind her neck and unsnapped the clasp for her. He turned back around to look away, and Delaney slowly slipped into the sweatshirt and pants while leaning onto the bed for balance. Thankfully, the pants had a drawstring that she was able to tie, though they were still too big. Then, she sat down feeling exhausted.

"Okay, I'm dressed," she said. She slowly moved to sit on the side of the bed to put the socks on, but Ben could see she was struggling.

"Let me help you," he said as he bent down on one knee and slipped a sock on each of her feet.

Ben pulled her to stand and helped her walk into the living room. He wasn't sure her legs would hold her yet. He started a fire in the wood-burning fireplace and then headed to the kitchen. "Don't move," he said.

Delaney was still shivering intermittently, partly from being cold and partly from leftover fear. Ben returned with a cup of hot tea and helped her take a few sips before he set it down on the coffee table. He sat down beside her and methodically wrapped his arms around her, pulling her to his chest.

"I know this may be awkward, but I need to keep your core warm," he said. Delaney wasn't complaining. It had been way too long since she'd been held by a man, especially one that looked and felt like him. He was warm and comforting, and he made her feel safe. She lay her head on his chest and inhaled his scent. He smelled of fresh soap and aftershave. Heat radiated from his body, and it warmed her.

She snuggled in closer to his chest. His breath was slow and gentle across her forehead. She was still shivering, but not as much. She could feel him wrap his arms around her tighter, as if he was saying something to her soul.

Ben felt his own core warming. Sensations he hadn't felt for a long time were springing up inside him. Being close to her almost felt natural, and he felt like he couldn't get close enough to her. He had forgotten how comforting a relationship with another human being could be. He had tried to push any emotion or feeling away, because feeling had brought him pain in the past. He had denied himself intimacy with another human being for so long. But in this moment, he found himself craving closeness.

She lifted her chin to look up at him. He was staring down at her, and his eyes were full of sadness. As she started to look down, he nudged her chin upward toward him. He looked at her lips and slowly leaned in toward her.

Delaney couldn't look away. Ben's lips almost brushed hers, but then something jolted Ben to an immediate halt. He pulled back from her and stared at her for a moment, as if he didn't recognize her. Then, he set her to his side and sat up. He plopped down off the couch onto the floor and said, "I think your core has warmed enough. Are you feeling better?"

Delaney felt dazed, as she tried to recover from the unexpected intimacy. She could see the strain in Ben's face. "Yes, thanks, Ben." She watched him a little longer, as he stared into the dancing, yellow and orange flames of the fire, lost in thought. "I'm not shivering anymore. Thank you for saving me," she said.

He let the words sink in while he stared at the fire. After a few moments, he looked up at her from his seated position on the floor, "Get some sleep. I'll be right here if you need me." Then, he stood up and covered her with a blanket.

Delaney didn't understand what was happening, but she guessed that he was probably upset with himself for almost making a pass at her. After all, they did have to work together. Any attempt at dating could turn out badly for both of them. *We just had a moment,* she thought. *And now it's passed.* "Good night, Ben," she whispered. Then, she added, "Sweet dreams."

After sitting by the fire for a while, Ben lay down on the rug beside the couch with a pillow and a blanket. He turned away from the couch on his side and stared at the fire. He liked Delaney. She was beautiful and smart. She seemed familiar, like home, but he didn't know why. He felt guilty for thinking about her. Wasn't it wrong to be thinking about a woman who wasn't his wife? He knew Danna was gone from this life forever, but his thoughts about Delaney made him feel like he was betraying Danna. Although he knew it was not a betrayal, it still felt like it. He hadn't thought about ever having another family or moving past his loss. He had just assumed it would be impossible. Strangely, though, his thoughts of Delaney made him feel something again.

Ben's thoughts began to blur as his eyelids became heavy. He glanced up at Delaney. She had been sleeping for a while. He hadn't slept well for eight years, but now, he was tired. He lay down on his pillow. A tear escaped from the corner of his eye. He missed Danna, but for the first time since losing her, Delaney had made him feel a little bit of hope. For the first time in eight years, he felt needed again. In the past, when he drifted off to sleep every night, the last face he always pictured in his mind was Danna's. Tonight, he could only see Delaney.

Chapter 8

Delaney opened her eyes when she sensed light in the room. Sunlight was shining through a nearby window. She started to move, but every muscle ached as if she'd done a core body workout the day before. As she became aware of her surroundings, she realized where she was, and the terror of the previous night returned. She slowly sat up. The fire was still burning in the fireplace. Ben must have stayed up most of the night keeping it going.

Ben … he had saved her life last night. She couldn't believe what had happened. How could she have been such an idiot? Why did she get so close to the side of the lake? The water really did look shallow, but then again, it was dark. Still, she knew better, and she was usually more cautious than that. She had just wanted to see what crazy person was out fishing at such an odd hour. *Wait, that must have been Ben in that boat. What was he doing out on the lake in the cold at night?* Then, she remembered the near-kiss. She took a deep breath as the thought gave her comfort. But she knew he had regretted it, and this made her feel bad, because she wasn't sure that she did. *It was one of those romantic moments,* she told herself. *We got caught up in the damsel in distress scenario. That's all.*

She heard a stirring sound on the floor beside her, and she peeked over the edge of the couch. Why was Ben sleeping on the floor? She stared at him while he slept. He looked peaceful. His breath was steady and even. The man was gorgeous, and today, he was more good-looking than ever. He had saved her life, and he had nearly kissed her. She shook her head as if to shake off the thought. The truth of the matter was that if he hadn't been in that boat out on the lake, she wouldn't be here, alive, now. She exhaled and looked at him again. His face was so gentle, yet so masculine. The morning stubble was evident and over-the-top handsome. She studied him some more. She could see lines in his face that she attributed to years of pain. She thought of his wife and daughter and felt a surge of pain in her heart for him. She studied his lips and, again, remembered the kiss they had almost shared just a few hours before. She wanted to replay it over and over.

He stirred, and Delaney quickly moved away from the edge of the couch.

Ben sat up and looked over at her. "Good morning," he said.

"Hi," she said feeling embarrassed. She knew she must be a mess right now, but he had seen her at her worst already.

"How are you feeling?" he asked.

"Grateful to you," she said.

He smiled, and this time, she could see dimples in both of his cheeks. *Oh my,* she thought, *and I didn't think he could get better looking.* Her face felt flushed and her stomach did a flop-flop, as she tried to fill the awkward moment with something else. Ben's defensive affect was gone this morning. He seemed lighthearted again, and she was glad to see it.

"By the way," she started, "I don't usually spend the night with men."

He smiled bigger and then chuckled. It was a happy sound to Delaney's ears. He replied with a lighthearted jab, "I get the feeling that you don't need a man in your life."

Delaney became serious for a moment, and her eyes started to tear up, "I did last night, and I wouldn't be here now if you hadn't saved me. Thank you for saving me."

He shook his head as if he had done nothing heroic, "You're welcome. I'm just glad I was there." Then, he added, "Promise me you won't take any more walks close to the lake alone at night?"

Delaney sighed and then smiled. She nodded. She was curious and asked, "Why were you out in a fishing boat on a cold night in the dark?"

Ben crawled over to the fireplace and poked at the logs using the fire iron. He added a few more logs and then moved back to his spot on the rug. He threw the blanket back over his legs. He looked at Delaney and said, "I go out there a lot at night, especially when the water is calm. It gives me a sense of peace, and I talk to God."

Delaney nodded her head, as if she understood. And she did. She replied, "I bet it's very peaceful."

"It is," he replied entering deep thought again. He chuckled to lighten things up and said playfully, "I should take you out on the lake sometime."

Delaney let out a big sigh and shook her head back and forth, "Not anytime soon. I'm going to stay away from the lake for a while. It tried to swallow me up last night!"

Ben stood up. He was wearing a white T-shirt with fleece pajama pants. Delaney could see every muscle in his chest and abdomen through the shirt. She had to look away because she felt her face flushing.

"How about some coffee?" he asked.

Delaney smiled and replied, "I so need coffee right now."

He said, "Stay there, and I'll bring it to you."

Delaney nodded as he disappeared into the kitchen. She was seeing Ben, as if for the first time. She didn't know this kind, playful, smiling Ben. Up until this point, she had only seen the hard core, heavy-hearted, stoic man. She liked this Ben, more than she wished to admit.

Ben returned from the kitchen a few minutes later with two coffee cups and a French press. "Oh, I love French press coffee," she said. Then, she added, "You like the fancy stuff, I see."

He smiled and replied, "It's the best." He poured two cups of coffee and handed one to Delaney.

She took a sip and looked out at the lake through the living room window. The sun was already up over the lake. She commented, "I bet you have beautiful sunrises here."

He looked out toward the lake and replied, "Almost every day. I love to take my coffee out on the front porch. It's beautiful. In fact, not too long ago, the sunrise looked almost purple. It was gorgeous."

Delaney nodded, "My mom used to call that a lavender sky. She told me it meant that good things were coming."

He looked at her and asked, "Where do your parents live?"

She told him the story of her parents and their deaths and that she really had no family left. He stared at her intently.

"What?" she asked.

"You must get lonely," he replied.

"Sometimes, the loneliness is too much to bear," she replied.

"I understand loneliness," he said, as he stared out the window.

She started to ask him about his past, but he interrupted, "I'm so sorry about your parents. I know that had to be hard for you and that it still is."

She replied, "Thank you. I sometimes wonder if the pain will ever ease." He didn't say anything, and she knew that he understood. She looked down at the clothes that hung off her petite frame and tried to lighten the mood, "So, you don't keep women's clothes in your house?"

He frowned and sighed deeply and said, "Not since my wife passed away."

Delaney took a deep breath and regretted her words. She could see the emotion in his face. She said, "I'm so sorry, Ben."

He stood up as if signaling that he didn't want to talk any-more. Delaney knew he was feeling uncomfortable and didn't want to talk about his past. "I'll be right back," he said. When he returned, he stretched his hands out to hand her something. "Here are your clothes," he said. "I dried them on low heat last night. You can change whenever you're ready, and then, I'll drive you to your car."

The change in his affect was immediate, and Delaney could see he was ready for her to go. The old Ben was back. She changed her clothes, and then, they hopped in his pickup truck, and he drove her to her car. When they drove up to her parked car, she pulled her keys out of her pocket. They sat in silence for a moment, as if neither of them knew what to say.

Delaney looked over at him and smiled. "Thanks again, Ben. I really owe you."

He hardly looked at her as if he was afraid to and replied, "I'm glad I was there. Take care, and see you around."

She opened the door and stepped out. As she closed the door, she smiled at him one last time.

This time he looked over at her. His eyes were full of sadness. He nodded his head and said, "See ya," and then, he glanced away. He put the truck in gear and watched her get into her car and start the engine; then, he drove away. Delaney sat still in her car for a moment processing the events of the night before. She recognized her blossoming feelings for Ben. "This is not wise," she said to herself as she put her car in gear and drove off.

Chapter 9

D elaney sat at her desk fidgeting with her pen. She placed a call, and after the fifth ring with no answer, she hung up the phone. She felt frustrated and worried. Savannah hadn't come to her last two appointments. Despite multiple attempts to reach Savannah by phone or letter, Delaney had been unable to talk to her. Why hadn't Savannah come to her appointments or at least answered her phone? Delaney couldn't help but fear the worst and uttered a prayer pleading with God to be with Savannah and help her. She had prayed the same prayer every night, and although she trusted God, she still worried that Savannah had made the choice to abort.

Delaney turned to look out the office window. The sun was rising, and the sun was lighting up the horizon. Delaney was mesmerized by the bold colors lighting up the sky before her. She felt a surge of peace come over her, as she decided to give this worry over to God. She knew she had to believe He would take care of Savannah and everything would be okay.

It was almost Christmas, but so far, there had been no snow. Delaney stared at the brown grass and naked tree branches outside. She missed the snow and didn't feel like winter or Christmas would be quite the same without it. The days had been cool, but not even cold. She had put up her Christmas tree and twinkle lights at home, but without the winter cold and snow, it felt almost like it wasn't right, like "Christmas in July" sales.

Despite the lack of snow, she loved what Christmas represented. For her, it was about remembering the birth of Jesus, being with family, and sitting by the fire on cold nights with loved ones, except that she didn't have anyone. She missed her mom and dad. Delaney exhaled and continued to stare out the window. The sun was up and in full force now. Despite the warmth through the window, her office still felt cold. She felt alone. As much as she loved Christmas, it was always a sad reminder of how lonely she was.

Delaney rose from her chair and walked into the hallway to start seeing patients. She pulled the chart from the first exam room door and was surprised and excited to see it was Savannah's chart. Her heart began racing, and she took a deep breath. What if she had aborted? Delaney inhaled a deep breath, as she tried to prepare herself for whatever she would find on the other side of the door. She turned the knob and entered the room and was greeted by Savannah and her 25-week-sized pregnant belly. Immediately, she let out a sigh of relief. She hadn't realized she was holding her breath. *Thank you, Lord,* she said as a silent prayer.

She smiled at Savannah and said, "I am so glad to see you." She rushed over to Savannah who was sitting on the exam table and hugged her. Then, she sat down on the stool beside her. Savannah actually smiled back as if she was taken off guard by such a warm greeting.

"I'm sorry I've missed my appointments. I haven't been able to call, because I've had to serve jail time."

Delaney's expression turned to concern, "Why? What happened?"

Savannah replied, "Oh, it's what I told you last time. I have court fees to pay for driving without a license. I have to serve so many days to pay off so much of the fine, since I don't have the money to pay for it."

Delaney asked, "Do you mind if I ask how much you owe?"

Savannah looked embarrassed but answered, "Yeah, I still owe about $900. I go back to jail next week, if I can't make a payment, and I can't."

Delaney asked, "What jail is it? The one here in Guntersville?"

Savannah looked down at the floor looking ashamed and replied, "Yeah."

Delaney changed the subject. "I'm proud of you," she said.

"What do you mean?" Savannah asked, looking up at her confused.

Delaney replied. "I know it took a lot of courage for you to make the decision to adopt your baby out."

Savannah took a deep breath and then said, "You know, Dr. Bartlett, I feel pretty sure that God put you in my life. I honestly don't believe in abortion, but before I met you, I couldn't see another answer. I was starting to feel hopeless, and then, you came along. I needed to hear someone tell me what to do. I think this might be God's way of helping me."

Tears came to Delaney's eyes, and she said, "Savannah I've been praying for you. I asked God to help you, and as you can see, He has good plans for you and this baby."

Delaney stood and hugged Savannah again, who was still perched up on the exam table. Delaney sat back down on the rolling stool with a big grin and asked, "So, have you chosen the adoptive parents?"

Savannah's smile lessened, and she responded with hesitation, "Well, I haven't signed with an adoption agency yet, but I've looked at several couple's profiles. I haven't found the right parents yet, but when I do, I'll sign with an agency. Once I do that, I'm told that it's supposed to be straightforward."

Delaney sensed the hesitation in Savannah's voice. Savannah could see Delaney's look of concern and said, "Don't worry, Dr. Bartlett. This baby is in God's hands, and I will know the right parents when it is time."

Delaney nodded and exhaled a big sigh and said, "You are so right."

Savannah left the office with an air of confidence and hope that day. Delaney could see it in her face. But, still, Delaney was troubled. When she had tried to schedule a follow-up visit for Savannah, Savannah told her she would have to wait.

She said, "I have to serve more jail time starting on Monday next week. I will just call for an appointment when I get out." Savannah had smiled so sweetly and humbly, as if she just accepted her consequences and was willing to pay the price.

Delaney felt dismayed. Savannah's platelets had dropped lower, and she needed frequent follow-up visits. Delaney sat in her office chair reviewing her conversation with Savannah that day. "How do I help her, Lord?" Delaney whispered.

Delaney's thoughts were interrupted as Candace poked her head through Delaney's half-opened door. She said, "Hey, Dr. B, here is a letter from the Guntersville Municipal Court. It looked like it might be important, so I brought it right away."

Delaney took the letter from Candace's extended hand. "Thanks," she said as Candace left.

Delaney tore open the envelope and read,

Dear Dr. Bartlett,

The Guntersville Municipal Court has been informed that you are the primary obstetrician for Miss Savannah Carter. Please be advised that she will be serving jail time until her court fees have been paid in full or until she has served her complete sentence. During this time, she will be absent from prenatal care. If there is a problem in the pregnancy, we will bring her to St. Jo's Medical Center North to receive care from you.

Sincerely,
David Andrew
Secretary to Judge Henry Davis

Delaney laid the letter on her desk, deep in thought. Maybe this was the answer she needed. She picked up her phone and dialed the number on the letter.

"Guntersville Municipal Court, this is David," answered a man's voice.

"Hi, this is Dr. Delaney Bartlett. I received a letter from you today about my pregnant patient, Savannah Carter," Delaney said.

"Yes, Dr. Bartlett. How can I help you?" David asked.

"Well," Delaney started, "I'd like to pay off Savannah's debt to the court."

There was a moment of silence. "This is a highly unusual request. You realize she's serving time for a crime?" he asked.

"Yes, I understand the situation completely, but I still want to pay it in full."

David commented, "That's very kind of you, Dr. Bartlett."

Delaney replied, "She has a high-risk pregnancy, and she really can't afford to miss getting prenatal care. So can I pay this debt with a credit card?"

David replied, "Sure, but do you know the total due is $1,020?"

Delaney replied, "Yes, I want to pay it, but with one condition. I don't want Savannah to know I paid it."

David agreed to her anonymity, and Delaney paid for it. Delaney hung up the phone. She sat motionless for a few moments as she stared out the window. The sky was gray now, and the temperature had dipped into the forties, but the sun was shining in Delaney's heart. "Thanks for showing me how to help, Lord," she whispered. She picked up the phone and called Candace, "Hey, lady. Would you please call Savannah Carter and be sure she has an appointment with me next week?"

"Sure thing, Dr. B," replied Candace.

Chapter 10

On Saturday, the week before Christmas, Delaney was off work. She headed to the local Piggly Wiggly to pick up some groceries. She planned to bake Christmas cookies on Christmas Eve, just as she did every year, and she wanted to go ahead and pick up the ingredients. This tradition had started with her mom, and she remembered at least two years of baking with her mom, at the ages of four and five. Her dad had carried on the tradition until Delaney's teenage years. Then, Delaney baked cookies every Christmas Eve on her own. Her favorite part with both of her parents had been decorating the cookies. This year, again, she would make her cookies alone; but she would turn on the Christmas lights, play Christmas music, and just remember the good times with her parents. It was a way for her to honor their memory.

As she pushed her cart around the corner of the last aisle, she was abruptly stopped as she ran into an oncoming shopper. After the cart completely stopped, and she saw that nothing had spilled out, she looked up to see if she had hurt the poor soul. Ben was staring back at her. He had one hand gripped on the front of the cart, while the other arm was holding a box of cereal, a loaf of bread, and a gallon of milk.

He slowly released his hand from the cart and said, "Hey Delaney, sorry about that." He seemed surprised to see her, and she was equally pleasantly surprised. She couldn't help but notice the massive size of his arms in his black tank top. His pectoral muscles were bulging toward her, and she decided she wouldn't mind touching them. He had on gym shorts that showed off his muscular legs.

"I'm sorry. I thought I had dropped something, and I turned around to look, but I should have stopped walking," he said. As he was talking, he motioned to replay what had happened. Delaney couldn't help but stare at him. She hadn't expected to see so much masculine skin in December.

"So you look like you're going to bake," he said.

Delaney was still staring at him.

"You are baking today?" He asked again, eyeing a response from her.

"Oh," she said snapping out of her daze. "Yes, how did you know?" she replied. She felt nervous, almost jittery. He pointed to her grocery basket filled with baking items. She looked down at her cart and said, "Oh right." Then, she looked at his clothes again and asked, "Isn't it a bit chilly to be dressed like that? It is December, you know."

He nodded and half smiled. "It's not snowing, and anyway, I just came from the gym. I'm going straight home, and I might take a swim in the lake." She glared up at him, and then, they both snickered. He looked at her cart again and said, "Looks like you're having a party, maybe for Christmas?"

Delaney smiled and replied, "No, just baking Christmas cookies by myself. It's one of my Christmas traditions. I used to do this every year with my parents, so it's something I do to make them feel closer."

He smiled at her and nodded again. "That's a really nice thing to do."

She looked at him with an inquiring eye and asked, "Are you going to see your parents for Christmas?"

He responded, "No." He hesitated and then added, "They live in San Diego. I prefer a quiet Christmas here."

She tilted her head to one side and raised one eyebrow and asked, "Alone?"

He nodded and said, "I like it that way."

Delaney exhaled a big sigh and said, "Well, if you change your mind and want company, you can come make Christmas cookies with me on Christmas Eve. I'll be alone too, and it would be fun to have a cookie co-conspirator."

He smiled big this time, and she could see his dimples. His deep brown eyes appeared to twinkle, and he said, "Cookie co-conspirator, huh? I've never been one of those before."

She smiled bigger at him and said, "Well, it will require that you actually decorate the cookies. You can't just be a bystander."

At that, he chuckled and said, "Maybe I'll stop by. Thanks."

She wrinkled her nose and said, "I'll start baking around five thirty, if you decide to come over."

She felt delirious after Ben walked away. Why did he have such an effect on her? She felt strangely connected to him and assumed it was because he had saved her life. But there was also the fact that she had spent the night at his house, but only by accident and out of necessity. Still, just the sight of him or being near him gave her comfort, like she had a soul connection with him. Her gleeful thoughts were short-lived as she frowned. She had a new problem. She liked him, a lot. She wondered if he might feel something for her. But what if he could not return her feelings? She assumed that friendship would be the best they could do, given his past pain, but she found herself wanting more. Was she falling in love?

Although his demeanor had been lighter toward her since the heroic deed, she reasoned that he was still guarded. Ben had a wall up and understandably so. His heart didn't seem open to her, or anyone for that matter. On occasion, like in the grocery store, she could see his heart open just a sliver, only to close again within moments. Because of this, she reasoned that he probably would not be coming over to help her bake cookies. She told herself that she was okay with that, but she really wasn't. While the thought of having him in her home and having his companionship for an evening lit up her heart, she forced herself to squelch that flame. It most likely wasn't going to happen.

She had spent the last few Christmas holidays with Pierce and his family. Although she had enjoyed having company at Christmas, his family concentrated more on their image. Their idea of a Christmas celebration was much different from hers. They would give an extravagant Christmas party inviting their socially elite friends. Delaney dreaded having to find a party dress for the big event each year. On top of that, Pierce usually wanted to "approve" of her choice of dress. He liked seeing her in elegant dresses, but each year, he liked a shorter and tighter one. She had started to feel like a trophy girlfriend for him to put on display.

Delaney just wanted to be home, next to the Christmas tree with a warm fireplace and good company. The one year she had asked Pierce to decorate cookies with her, he had spent the majority of his time on his phone. She had been prepared to be alone for this Christmas and had been okay with it. She even preferred being alone to being with Pierce and his family. But this year, she hoped Ben would be with her. She sighed.

Ben smiled as he walked to his car in the Piggly Wiggly parking lot. The sight of Delaney made him feel happy. He hadn't expected to feel such a surge of emotion. The fact that she had asked him to spend Christmas Eve with her baking cookies gave him a burst of confidence. A beautiful woman wanted to spend time with him. His usual empty self felt a little fuller, though he wasn't sure what he should do. Ever since the lake incident with Delaney, he hadn't been able to stop thinking about her. Granted, he had really tried not to think about her, but her sweet smile kept showing up in his mind. He couldn't forget the feel of her slender body next to his when he had held her. She had been vulnerable and weak in his arms. He hadn't seen that side of her before. She had always seemed so tough and sure of herself. She created a longing in him that he hadn't felt since losing Danna. The part of him that felt guilty for wanting to spend time with Delaney was still there, but he believed that maybe the guilt would lessen if he would just try. Maybe it was time for him to take a chance and take a step forward.

Chapter 11

T he rest of the week seemed to last forever for Delaney. She couldn't stop wondering if Ben would come over to make cookies. She imagined him in her kitchen spending time with her, and she could feel her heart swell. She had seen him in the OR that week and had been looking for some kind of clue as to what he was thinking, but he had been a man of few words.

When Christmas Eve arrived, Delaney awoke early that morning. She peeked out the window hoping to see snow. "Fat chance," she said. Then, she added, "Well, it never hurts to hope. At least, it's cold enough for snow." She and Finn had split coverage for the Christmas holiday. Finn was taking call today, and she would be covering the hospital tomorrow on Christmas Day. She felt excited as she bounced to the kitchen to brew some coffee. After the morning when Ben served her French press coffee, she had gone out and bought a French press. That's how she had made her coffee since Ben, and she enjoyed it even more. It seemed more comforting, and she was sure it was because it made her thoughts return to Ben.

"I think I need some strawberry muffins this morning for Christmas Eve," she announced. She looked up at the ceiling and said, "Mom and Dad, these muffins are for you." She smiled as she turned on some Christmas music. She prepared the muffins while rocking out to Elvis singing *Blue Christmas*. When she pulled the baked muffins from the oven, she immediately plopped one on a plate. She smeared some butter on it and enjoyed the wonderful berry flavor of each bite. She washed it down with a fresh cup of coffee and then made a list of things she needed to do.

As she glanced around the house, she decided the first thing she would do was straighten up, just in case Ben decided to come over. She wanted to give him the impression that she was a fairly neat and clean person. By 2:30 p.m., the house was clean, but Delaney's energy was waning. A migraine headache was setting in. She popped a sumatriptan tablet in her mouth and swallowed it down with a glass of water. Unfortunately, she hadn't caught the headache in time, and her pain worsened. She knew she would have to lie down for a while.

She set her alarm for 4:30 p.m., knowing she would need an hour to get ready if Ben came over. Then, she lay down. Sleep was not going to come easily, since the pain in her temple and behind her eye was intensifying. She got up and grabbed an ice pack from the freezer. She lay back down and placed the ice pack on her head.

Delaney wanted to curse herself for missing her migraine aura this time. She was accustomed to getting migraines and knew when they were coming on and how long it would take for the medicine to work. Usually, she could catch her headache at the first twinge of pain in her left temple. Today, she had failed miserably at the identification-of-migraine stage and had waited too long to take her medicine, so she knew it would take more time for the medicine to work.

At one point, the pain had become so bad that she crawled up into a fetal position. After thirty minutes of worsening pain, she took a second dose of medicine along with her anti-nausea medicine. She knew nausea was coming next. Her headaches had started in her second year of medical school. She had gone to the ER the first time, and once she had received a diagnosis, she was able to self-diagnose when future headaches presented. She was grateful to have prescription medicine to treat her headaches, so she could avoid ER visits.

Delaney awoke to the doorbell and her alarm. It was almost dark outside, with very little daylight left. She felt groggy, but the pain in her head was gone. It took her a few seconds to realize what day it was and what was going on. She heard the doorbell chime again.

"Oh no!" she exclaimed, as she turned off her alarm. It had been beeping for an hour, and she hadn't heard it. She stood up out of bed, but felt off-balance. "Oh my gosh," she said as she realized that she was in her pajamas with bed head and awful breath, and Ben was probably at the door. For a second, she thought she might not answer the door. *Maybe he'll just go home,* she reasoned. But then again, that's not what she wanted.

She ran to the front door. The front porch light and her outdoor Christmas lights weren't even on. She opened the door, but didn't see anyone. She looked toward her driveway, and Ben's truck lights came on. He was leaving. He must have figured she wasn't home. Delaney was freezing in her bare feet and pajamas, but she ran down the sidewalk toward his truck so he would see her.

She ran over to his window waving, and he rolled it down.

"Hey," she said.

Before she could say anything else, he said, "Hey, sorry. I'm guessing you're busy. I'll just go. I don't want to bother you."

She gave him a look of concern and said, "Oh my gosh, Ben, I'm so sorry. I had a migraine today, and I had to take a nap. My alarm has been going off for an hour. I didn't wake up until I heard the doorbell. Please stay and come in."

Ben looked at her and said, "I get migraines too. I totally get it. Are you sure you want company?"

Delaney exhaled, "Yes, please. I would love some company. We have to make cookies, remember, Mr. Co-conspirator?"

Ben turned off the engine and said, "Get inside before you catch a cold. I'll be right in."

Chapter 12

D elaney turned on the outdoor Christmas lights when she went inside. The two columns on the front porch were wrapped spirally in white twinkle lights. There was a life-size nativity scene in the front yard that lit up with white lights, and on the front door hung a large, lit Christmas wreath. Ben walked through the front door after knocking. Delaney had left it open for him. He walked into the entry and saw the twinkling Christmas tree next to the fireplace. Delaney had turned on the gas fireplace. The house felt cozy. He walked to the kitchen and set down the thermos he was carrying on the counter.

Delaney was in her bedroom trying to make herself presentable. She yelled out to the kitchen, when she heard Ben come in, "Just make yourself comfortable, and I'll be right out."

She was surprised when Ben peeked around the corner, right after she yelled from her bedroom. "Oh sorry, I didn't realize you were so close."

Ben said, "You don't need to change out of your pajamas. I'm sure those are the most comfortable things for you right now." Delaney started to argue, but then Ben said, "Besides, you look really cute, and I've seen you in less."

Delaney stared at him for a moment with a smirk on her face, as she registered what he had said. *He is flirting with me,* she thought. Then, she smiled and nodded and said, "Okay, thanks. I'll be right there." She brushed her hair and her teeth and applied a little makeup and then hurried out to the kitchen to get the cookies started.

Once in the kitchen, she saw that Ben had found and set out two coffee mugs. He was pouring something from a thermos into the mugs. He had pulled out all of the ingredients for the cookies, and the oven was even preheating.

"I'm seeing a man in my kitchen who looks too comfortable with the baking supplies and tools. I'm thinking you've been putting on an act for me. You really are a serious baker, aren't you?" Delaney observed.

He smiled at her and said, "I take my cookie co-conspirator role very seriously." They both laughed. "Have a seat," he said, as he handed her a coffee mug.

Delaney took the mug and sniffed it. "Is this hot chocolate?" she asked.

"Yes, it's my mom's recipe. She adds a pinch of chili powder, and it gives the flavor a nice kick. It will warm you from the inside out."

She smiled at him and then took a careful sip. She blinked her eyes and shook her head slightly. "Wow, I see what you mean. It's really good. I think the chili powder makes the chocolate flavor seem richer," she said. "This will go great with the cookies."

"Oh, you mean I get to eat them too? I'm not just the cookie co-conspirator?" he asked with a smirk on his face.

She shook her head at him, smiling. She was thrilled to have Ben in her kitchen. He looked good. He wore a green sweater with dark blue jeans and black boots. The jeans fit him perfectly, and the sweater fit just right showing his broad shoulders and chiseled body. The man was incredibly attractive. Her thoughts were interrupted as Ben turned toward her while wrapping an apron around his waist. Delaney could hardly handle the sight of him.

He smiled at her playfully and asked, "So what exactly is my job as a cookie co-conspirator?"

Delaney appreciated his lighthearted humor right now. Her migraine medicine always left her with a groggy hangover, and she was still trying to feel more alert.

"Well," she started.

He interrupted her when he could see how tired she looked. "Have a seat right here," he said as he motioned to a bar stool at the counter. He walked over and pulled the chair out. Delaney sat down obeying his command. "Here," he said as he slid her hot chocolate toward her. Then, he raised his eyebrows and smiled at her, "Where is your rolling pin?"

Delaney could see that he had already put the ingredients together in a bowl for sugar cookies. He was mixing them together and ready to roll out the dough. She said, "How did you do that so fast?"

He playfully answered, "I know my way around the kitchen."

Delaney walked over to the cabinet to pull out the rolling pin. As she did, she brushed against Ben. *Oh my,* she thought to herself. She could use more close encounters like that one. She handed him the rolling pin, and before she knew it, the first batch of cookies was baking.

"Where is that Christmas music you mentioned the last time I saw you?" he asked.

Delaney smiled and held up her index finger as if to say, "One moment." She tapped on her iPod until *The Christmas Song* could be heard playing.

After several batches of cookies were baked and had cooled, Ben and Delaney sat down together to decorate them. The Christmas music continued to play softly in the background.

"Man, you're pretty serious about this decorating business," he said as he looked at the table.

"Yes, every year, I use the same cookie cutters and types of decorations." Delaney replied. Then, she paused and held up her arm motioning like Vanna White on *Wheel of Fortune,* "Over here, we have three different cookie frostings in the festive colors of red, green, and white." She smiled and motioned to the other side of the table, "Over here, we have every kind of festive sprinkle you can imagine." Then, she motioned to the far end of the table, "And over there, we have our icing writing tools in silver, white, green, and red."

Ben just shook his head and looked at the spread of decorations, "I'm impressed. I can't say that I've ever met a more organized or thorough cookie decorator. It is truly an honor to be your cookie co-conspirator tonight."

They both chuckled, and then, Delaney looked at him seriously. "Thanks for doing this with me. It's nice to have company for this. I really miss my mom and dad."

Ben pursed his lips and then smiled, "Glad I can help. It's nice for me, too. I'm usually alone. I mean, I don't mind it, but it's a nice change of pace to have something fun to do for the holidays."

The two of them sat silently decorating cookies. Delaney looked up a few times asking Ben to pass the sprinkles or icing over. Ben remained quiet. It was odd to Delaney, but the silence was comfortable. She was accustomed to the silence and assumed he was too, but this was different because this silence was shared.

As the last cookie was complete, Ben stood from his chair to admire their work. "You're quite the artist," he said.

"I was just about to say the same thing to you. I think you've done this before," she said tilting her head and raising an eyebrow.

Their eyes met, and an awkward silence followed. It was the first real awkward moment of the night. Ben's eyes locked onto hers, and he felt something he had never felt for anyone other than Danna. He felt connected to her. This woman was getting to him. She looked so darn cute in her pajamas, and he was really struggling to keep himself from taking her into his arms and kissing her. He wanted to, but he couldn't.

Delaney felt her heart racing. The look on Ben's face told her he was looking into her heart. His face was filled with sadness and loneliness, and she understood that. She was tired of being alone. She felt entranced by his eyes, but the more she thought of him, the more she wanted to step closer to him, to be in his arms. She became aware of her face starting to feel flushed, and she became embarrassed. She broke his stare and looked away wanting to escape her discomfort. "Would you like something to eat?" she asked, feeling the need to fill the awkward moment with conversation.

Ben seemed to be lost in thought, still looking at her. He knew he had to escape now. His resolve to not take her into his arms was melting away. The pull he felt to be close to her was overpowering. He looked away and said, "Oh, no thanks. It's late. I need to get going."

Delaney felt disappointed. "Are you sure? How about some popcorn and a movie?"

"No, I can't. I mean, I have an early morning tomorrow. I should go." Ben's affect had changed. He was no longer comfortable, nor did he have that yearning look in his eyes. Instead, he looked like he wanted to leave as quickly as possible.

He headed toward the door, and Delaney followed him. He grabbed his coat and was walking off the porch before he said another word. He turned still walking away and said, "Thanks. I had fun."

Delaney could see his wall had been put up, and it had gone up fast. "Bye," she yelled after him. "Thanks for coming over. I had a great time."

Ben didn't dawdle. He was pulling out of her driveway in seconds. He waved to her, and then, he was gone.

Delaney closed the door feeling disappointed. She wanted him to stay longer. She leaned against the closed door for a few moments. Had she said or done something to make him want to run away? She couldn't figure it out beyond their awkward stare. The evening had been fun and easy with him, up until those last few moments. She stared at the floor and then rolled her eyes as she realized her attraction to him was undeniable. She couldn't help it. He was gorgeous—those big brown eyes, his Superman curl, his chiseled jawline, those full lips, and that muscular build. She knew that her attraction was not just physical. Aside from the fact that he was eye candy, he had also saved her life. He was a good man with a kind heart, and he had a heart for God. He was everything she had always wanted in a man.

She let out a deep sigh. That sadness in his eyes was there every time she looked at him. Her heart ached for him. She had heartache from losing her parents, and she felt pain from being dumped so cruelly by Pierce, so she could relate a little. But she couldn't imagine losing a spouse and young child and so tragically. He'd had no closure, no goodbye, just torment. Tears collected in her eyes as she imagined the pain he must feel. She looked to the ceiling and uttered a small prayer, "Lord, please give Ben strength and bring him joy again."

She wiped a tear from her cheek and realized how tired she was. She cleaned the kitchen and then brushed her teeth and crawled into bed.

Chapter 13

Ben drove home the long way around the lake. He had enjoyed the evening with Delaney, and it felt good to have companionship again. He had become accustomed to being alone, but tonight, being with Delaney had filled a void. At the same time, it made him realize just how lonely he was. It didn't sit well with him, and he couldn't stop thinking about it. He missed Danna and Ella, and now that he wanted to feel some comfort from Delaney, he still could feel nothing but misery. The ache in his heart was supposed to lessen with time, not grow.

When he arrived at home, he took his boat out. It was cold, but the lake was still. The sky was clear and dotted with an array of twinkling lights. The moon shone full and lit up the waters, casting the light of thousands of candles. Ben turned off the motor and dropped the anchor out. He sat in silence staring up at the bright sky. Within a few seconds, tears erupted and spilled down his cheeks.

"Lord, I miss them. Please help me. My heart hurts so much. I thought being with Delaney would lessen my pain and loneliness tonight, but it didn't. I still feel the tearing pain of their loss all over again. I can't live like this. Please give me strength."

Ben couldn't hold back the sobs. After a few moments of crying, the release of the emotions made him feel better. He remembered one of God's promises from Isaiah 41:10, "Do not fear, for I am with you, do not be dismayed, for I am your God. I will strengthen you and help you. I will uphold you with my righteous right hand." As hard as it was to believe right now, Ben decided to keep clinging to that truth. His only other choice would be to give up, and he knew he couldn't do that.

He sat for a few more moments thinking of Delaney. She was beautiful with her long, wavy brown hair and green eyes. Her smile melted his heart, and her laugh was contagious. He hadn't planned on ever feeling anything for any woman other than Danna. These feelings were new and scary for him. He couldn't help but feel as if he was betraying the memory of Danna by having feelings for Delaney. He couldn't forget Danna or his love for her. Although he knew she was gone, he still felt her with him. He wouldn't dishonor her memory.

The next morning, on Christmas Day, Ben arose early before sunrise. He hadn't slept well. He made coffee with his French press and sipped it in silence. He looked around the house. It was a small lake house. The living room and kitchen were small but had all of the modern necessities. A small bar counter between the kitchen and living room was his kitchen table. There were two bar stools, though he rarely used both of them. Down a back hall, there was one bathroom and two bedrooms. When Ben had moved in, he had just wanted a small place on the lake.

Seclusion was important for him, and he had it here. There were a few other lake houses in the area, but the homes were scattered far apart. Ben liked that, because he didn't want to be disturbed or have to chat with neighbors. He wasn't antisocial, but he didn't like small talk.

He sat at the kitchen bar finishing his coffee. He looked around the living room. The room was minimally furnished with just a couch, a coffee table, and a rocking chair. The fireplace was built of creek stone and took up an entire wall. The wood floor had rugs sprinkled over it to add warmth. Ben's eyes landed on the only picture in his living room. It was a picture of Danna holding Ella, when she was an infant.

"I miss you so much," he said softly. A tear escaped his eye and rolled off his cheek. He sniffled and wiped his eyes with his hand. In the eight years since the funeral, he had not gone back to their grave sites. It had been too painful. He believed that by visiting their grave sites, he would have been admitting that he had accepted their deaths. He could not accept that they were gone, and he wouldn't.

Until Delaney had come into his life, he had thought of them every minute. Delaney had helped him smile again, even laugh, but it didn't feel right. Was Delaney really in his life? He wasn't sure, but he did know that she was taking up room in his thoughts, whether he liked it or not. Guilt pained him as he realized that he had feelings for her. He hadn't planned this. He couldn't let himself fall for her.

He slowly walked over to the rocking chair, dragging his feet, looking like a defeated man. He picked up a small, stuffed bear and then sat down in the chair, still holding the bear. The bear had been Ella's, and his name was Boo. Other than pictures of Ella, it was the only possession of Ella's he had brought to Alabama. The rest of her things were in storage, along with Danna's. He hadn't been able to go through any of their things after the accident, so his friends had boxed up their belongings for him and put them in a storage unit back in San Diego.

He rocked in the chair and stared at the picture. Danna used to sit in this same chair and rock Ella to sleep. He had rocked Ella to sleep in this chair. Ben knew he would never be the same happy man he had once been, not without Danna and Ella. The memories were too painful, and the loss had changed him forever. He no longer lived with a purpose. Danna and Ella had been his life. He had lived to provide for them and be a husband and father. Ben didn't know who he was without them. He felt lost and without a compass. "Why am I still here, Lord?" He asked, looking out the window toward the sky.

He stood from the rocking chair, still staring out at the sky. He shook his head back and forth and, with resolve, he said, "I can't spend time with Delaney anymore." Then, he added, "I'm sorry, Danna."

Chapter 14

C hristmas Day had been quiet and lonely for Delaney. Candace had invited her over, but Delaney didn't feel like socializing. She was glad to be back at the office the next day. She noticed that Finn wasn't in yet, but she figured he was enjoying a little more time with his family. She sat at her desk reviewing lab results and patient phone messages.

Candace popped her head through Delaney's half-opened door. "Good morning."

Delaney looked up, "Good morning. How was your Christmas?"

Candace smiled and replied, "Oh, it was wonderful. The boys were so happy with what Santa brought. We had my family over for Christmas dinner. I was hoping you would make it over."

Delaney smiled, "Well, I wanted a quiet day. I watched *It's a Wonderful Life* and *Elf* and ate some Christmas cookies. I got some much needed rest."

Candace said, "Well, I made some fresh coffee, if you want some. I also brought in some blueberry muffins. They are in the kitchen. Also, Dr. Donovan called in sick. He said he won't be able to make it in today."

"Did he say what was wrong?" asked Delaney.

"He said he thinks he has the flu," replied Candace.

"Okay, thanks. I hope he is okay. I guess you'll have to add his obstetric patients to my schedule and reschedule the gynecology patients." Delaney knew her day had just been lengthened, and she sighed.

"Dr. Bartlett, I know this is not my business, but he's been out a lot lately. You have to be tired of carrying his load," Candace said.

"I'm okay, Candace. Thanks. I think I'll come have some of your coffee and a muffin. It's exactly what I need right now," Delaney replied, forcing a smile.

Delaney rose from her chair and headed to the kitchen. The kitchen smelled of fresh coffee and muffins like a bakery. "Mmmm," Delaney said. She poured a cup of coffee, added cream, and grabbed a blueberry muffin and headed back to her office. She sat down to eat her muffin. Candace was right. Finn had been missing a lot of work. Delaney had also noticed that when he was at the office, he would leave frequently for long periods of time. He would eventually return, but he was leaving patients to wait for too long. Another odd behavior to hit her radar recently was that medical records had started to call her complaining that Finn wasn't completing his charts. They had asked her to talk with him, which she hadn't gotten around to yet. Come to think of it, Finn had recently missed a delivery because the nurses couldn't get in touch with him. Something had to be going on with him.

She reviewed the rest of the charts stacked on her desk and was about to get up when the phone rang.

"Hello," she answered.

"Good morning, Dr. Bartlett. This is Griffin Jones," the voice said.

Griffin was the CEO of the hospital and had helped to recruit her there. She felt sudden anxiety as to why he might be calling. "Hi Griffin," she replied. After some small talk, she asked him, "Did you have a nice Christmas?"

"Yes, it was wonderful. How was yours?" he replied.

"Oh, it was pretty festive. When I wasn't on call, I made some cookies and watched some classic Christmas movies. It was a cozy Christmas," she said. After a pause, she asked, "What can I do for you, Griffin?"

He replied, "I was wondering if you have a few minutes to talk today. I could come by this afternoon."

"Sure," she replied. "Can you stop by at four thirty?"

"Yes, that works. I'll be there," said Griffin.

Griffin was waiting for Delaney in her office at 4:30 p.m. Delaney walked in after seeing her last patient. "Hi, Griffin," she said with a cheerful smile.

Griffin stood and shook her hand, "Good to see you, Dr. Bartlett. Thanks for meeting with me."

"Of course, Griffin. Please call me Delaney," she replied. She removed her white coat and draped it across her office chair. Then, she took a seat across the desk from Griffin. Delaney observed Griffin. He was a tall man of about six feet when standing. He was middle-aged, probably about forty-seven or forty-eight and had black hair with streaks of gray. His eyes were deep blue, and he had a kind face.

He smiled at her but had concern in his eyes. He wasn't here for small talk or a friendly visit. "I guess you're wondering why I want to talk with you," he said.

"Yes," she replied. "I figured it must be important, since you didn't want to discuss it on the phone earlier today."

He paused, as if he wasn't sure how to start. Then, he proceeded, "I've been getting a lot of complaints about Dr. Donovan from the nursing staff, other doctors, and medical records."

"What kind of complaints?" asked Delaney.

"The nursing staff has repeatedly told me that they have trouble reaching Dr. Donovan on his cell phone. He even missed a recent delivery because he wouldn't answer his phone. When they finally reached him, he said that he had been sleeping and hadn't heard the call. The anesthesiologists and OR staff are fed up with him because he is always late for his surgeries. They took away the early morning surgery slot from him last week, because he can't get to the hospital on time, and that puts their whole schedule behind. Medical Records has called me at least twice a month for the last three months telling me that he has not done several dictations nor has he signed any charts over the last sixty days." Griffin stared at her for any insight; then he added, "Have you observed any of this, or has he said anything to you?"

"Wow," was all Delaney could manage initially. Then, she added, "No, he hasn't said anything to me. I've noticed that he's been a little more aloof in the last month. I haven't seen him in the office as much, because he's been out sick quite a bit. Plus, I've noticed that he's been leaving almost every day during office hours. He leaves for an hour or so and then returns. Candace has come to me saying that the patients are complaining about their wait. I've even seen some of those patients for him. I have to admit that I've also heard a few snide remarks from the OR nurses about how he is late a lot." She paused and then said, "Something isn't right for sure. In residency, he was always behind with his medical records, so that doesn't surprise me. But he was not absent or sick, and he always answered his phone."

"Do you think you could talk to him?" Griffin asked.

"Sure," she said. "I'd be glad to. I'm concerned anyway. We're old friends, and I need to be sure everything is okay. I'll talk to him next time I see him."

"Thanks, I really appreciate it, Delaney," replied Griffin. He stood and shook her hand and said, "I'll let you get back to your work. Talk to you soon."

Delaney pursed her lips and nodded at him, as Griffin walked out.

She stared at the wall in her office for a few moments. Finn was showing bad form right now. It didn't make sense. Obstetricians had to be responsible doctors. One missed phone call could mean a missed delivery or a missed emergency. Patients' lives were on the line, and they depended on the doctor to be available at all times. It wasn't fair to the patients or the nursing staff. He was setting himself up to be a liability by not being available. Finn knew this. Delaney was also growing weary of seeing his patients. He had been "out sick" too much, and where was he going during these middle-of-office excursions? Something had to be going on.

Chapter 15

Delaney got in her car and started the engine. She had decided to go visit Finn after talking to Griffin. It was almost 6:00 p.m. She dialed Finn's number, but he didn't answer. Delaney had agreed to cover the hospital call that night for him, since he was sick. So when he didn't answer, it made sense to her that he was probably resting. She called his house phone, thinking his wife would answer, but there was no answer.

She decided to drive over and check on him. Finn had rented a house in her neighborhood about a mile away. She stopped there on her way home and was surprised that no cars were there. She got out of her car and walked to the front door. She rang the doorbell and waited. There was no stirring or noise inside that she could hear. She rang the doorbell again. Still nothing. She hoped he was all right, as she got back in her car and drove home.

The next morning at the office, Finn arrived late. He was supposed to start seeing patients at eight o'clock, but he didn't walk through the door until ten o'clock Delaney walked to his office. The door was closed, which was odd, because he never closed the door. She knocked.

"Come in," she heard him say.

Delaney turned the knob, but it was locked. Why would he need to lock his door? She knocked again saying, "It's locked."

Finn was at the door right away and had it open for her. "Oh sorry," he said. "I was on an important phone call, and it was private."

"No problem," she replied. "Can I talk to you for a minute?"

"Sure," he said smiling. "Have a seat." He motioned for her to sit in a chair across from his desk.

Delaney sat down and looked at him. He looked tired. He had dark circles under his eyes, and his appearance was disheveled. The lines in his face had deepened over the last month, and he looked skinnier. "You don't look so good," she said. "What's going on with you?"

Finn took a deep breath and then took a big swig of his Red Bull drink. He said, "Well, I've had the flu."

"Yes, I know, and I hope you're feeling better. But there's more, Finn. I'm your friend. I know there is more." She waited for him to say something, but he didn't. She continued, "Some bizarre stuff has been happening lately, and I hope you'll confide in me as to what's going on. Something is up, and I know it. You're not answering your phone when you're on call, you missed a delivery last week, the OR staff is complaining about how you are always late for surgery, Medical Records is frustrated because you're not doing your dictations or signing your charts, and you're disappearing from the office for hours at a time while you're patients are waiting. I've had to see several of your patients on top of my already busy schedule. Last night, I stopped by your house to check on you, and you weren't home. Are you in some kind of trouble?"

Finn looked away and took another gulp of Red Bull; then, he let out a big breath and said, "I didn't want to tell anyone, but I'm going through a divorce. Sabrina has a drug addiction, and I've been trying to cover for her. I don't want a divorce, but she does. It's probably for the best since she won't get help, and she's ruining my life."

Delaney's eyes widened, and her mouth gaped open. She covered it with her hand in shock. "Oh, Finn, I'm so sorry. I had no idea. How long has this been going on?"

He replied, "About six months. When we moved here a year ago, she was a recovered opiate addict. She didn't want to move here. I think the move and the fact that she misses her friends and family caused her to use again. She left me and moved in with her parents a few weeks ago."

Delaney wasn't sure what to say. She remained quiet for a minute and then asked, "How can I help you?"

He answered, "You can't really, except to be supportive. I might need some help with call or seeing patients occasionally, but I'm going to try to do my part."

Delaney sat back in her chair, "Of course, I will do what I can to help. Do you already have a lawyer involved? Have you two considered counseling? I mean, what's your next move?"

He looked down at his desk and took another swig of his Red Bull finishing off the can. "We are way past counseling, and she has called a lawyer. I'm waiting for her to file papers."

It struck Delaney as odd that although Finn seemed to recognize that his marriage was ending and that this was a bad situation, he seemed extremely calm and unconcerned. He had smiled too much during the conversation, and he couldn't seem to get enough of his Red Bull. Something was off about his affect, but she couldn't pin it down.

She stood and said, "Well, you know I'm here for you. I think you should let Griffin know what's happening. He came by yesterday. He was concerned."

"I'll call him today," he replied.

"You promise you'll call him?" she asked.

"Yes, I promise. Thanks for your help," he said.

Delaney nodded with hesitation and left his office.

A few weeks later at the end of January, Delaney sat in her office reviewing labs. Candace knocked on her door and asked, "Dr. Bartlett, can I come in?"

Delaney looked up and smiled, "Sure. Have a seat."

Candace closed the door and sat down. She looked scared.

"What's wrong?" Delaney asked leaning forward in her chair.

Candace looked around to be sure the door was closed, and she leaned forward and whispered, "The sheriff is in Dr. Donovan's office."

Delaney's eyes widened and her face expressed shock. "What?" she asked in the same quiet voice Candace used. "Why? What's going on?"

"I don't know, but it's freaking me out. The sheriff was all serious, and he closed the door when he went in there."

87

Delaney arose from her seat and opened her office door. She walked out into the hallway with Candace following her. Finn's door was still closed, and she could hear them talking. Delaney and Candace wandered to the front desk area. The waiting room was calm, and the patients seemed to be fine. Delaney looked up when she heard Finn's door open and saw the sheriff coming out. The sheriff acknowledged Delaney and nodded and tipped his hat to her without saying anything. He left through the waiting room.

"Stay here," she said to Candace. Delaney walked to Finn's office expecting to find him sitting at his desk. Instead, he was gone. She backtracked and looked in her office and the kitchen. Then, she looked in the lab and the bathroom. No Finn. He had left.

"He's gone," Delaney said to Candace.

"I wonder what that was all about," she said.

"It couldn't have been good," replied Delaney with an exasperated look on her face.

"Dr. Donovan has five OB patients to see still. What do I tell them?" Candace whined.

"I'll see them. Tell them Dr. Donovan had an emergency, and if they will wait a bit, I will see them today," Delaney sighed.

"Okay," said Candace, and she disappeared into the waiting room.

Delaney went to her office and closed the door. She picked up the phone and called Griffin's office.

Sally, his assistant, answered, "Griffin Jones' office, this is Sally. How can I help you?"

"Hi, Sally. This is Dr. Bartlett. Is Griffin in? I really need to speak with him now."

"Sure, Dr. Bartlett, just one moment, and I'll transfer you," she replied.

Griffin answered his phone within seconds, "Hey, Delaney. What can I do for you?"

Delaney told Griffin about Finn's visit by the sheriff and how Finn had left the office right after the visit without saying a word to anyone. Then, she added, "Something must be wrong."

Griffin asked, "Did you ever get a chance to talk to him and find out what's been going on with him?"

Delaney was confused. "Yes, I talked to him right after you came to my office. It was right after Christmas. Finn told me he would call you and talk to you. I assumed he did."

Griffin answered, "No, he never called me."

Delaney exhaled and shook her head in frustration. Then, she proceeded to relay the discussion she had with Finn to Griffin. She added, "Although his story seemed to fit the issues with his behavior, something about him was off that day. He seemed too happy-go-lucky given the fact that his wife had a drug addiction and was leaving him. He didn't look good either. He looked tired, skinny, and disheveled. He seems worse over these last few weeks."

Griffin sighed loudly, "I'll talk to him. I'm also going to call the sheriff to see if he'll tell me anything. This whole situation is disturbing. Thanks for letting me know, Delaney."

"Sure," she replied. "Let me know if I can do anything. I'm going to see his patients today."

They disconnected the line. Delaney had a bad feeling, but she couldn't imagine what was going on for sure. Maybe Sabrina had caused a scene with the neighbors. Maybe the sheriff had arrested her. Delaney enjoyed being a law-abiding citizen and didn't like being this close to a problem with law enforcement. But something was happening right here in her neck of the woods.

Chapter 16

Two weeks later, Delaney was seeing Savannah for an office visit. She was now thirty-two weeks pregnant and doing well. She had been able to keep all of her prenatal visits so far, and she seemed a little happier. Savannah had told Delaney how the court had mysteriously dismissed her charges, and she was elated to not have to serve more jail time. Delaney had acted surprised and relieved for Savannah at the news.

Delaney held a paper up and then looked at Savannah and said, "Your platelet count is seventy-two. That's low."

Savannah asked, "So what does that mean?"

Delaney answered, "I would like to put you in the hospital for a few days so I can run some tests and treat you with a course of steroids. I worry that the baby may need to be delivered a little early because of your platelets, and the steroids will help to mature your baby's lungs."

"She might come early?" Savannah asked. She then added, "Will she be okay?"

"Yes," replied Delaney. "The steroids will help to speed up maturity of her lungs, brain, and gut. If she doesn't need to be delivered early, the steroids still won't hurt her."

Savannah seemed worried, "Well, you're the doctor, and I trust you, so I'll do whatever you want me to."

"Thanks for trusting me, Savannah," Delaney said. "I'm going to fax some orders over to labor and delivery. Go ahead and go home to pack some clothes and toiletries and then check in at the labor and delivery desk. They will be expecting you."

Savannah left, and Delaney finished seeing patients. She sat down in her office to answer phone messages, and her phone rang.

"Hello?" she said.

"Hey, Delaney. This is Griffin. Are you busy?" Griffin asked.

"No, I'm just finishing up here in the office. What's up?" Delaney asked.

Griffin said, "I wanted to follow up with you on that sheriff incident at your office a few weeks ago."

"Oh right. Well, I asked Finn about it, and he told me that his wife forgot to pay their rent for two months in a row. He said that he wrote a check to the sheriff, and that was it," Delaney commented.

Griffin was silent and exhaled loudly. "Well, I believe that is partially true, because his rent did go unpaid for a couple of months. But there is more. The thing is, I can't say anything else right now, and I'm asking you to not say anything else to Finn. There is a police investigation going on, and the less you and I know right now, the better."

Delaney's eyebrows shot upward in shock, "Okay," she said. "You are scaring me, Griffin."

"No need to be scared. I'm guessing it has something to do with his wife. The sheriff asked us to watch for weird behaviors in Finn or strange activity and to let them know," Griffin said.

Delaney shook her head and said, "Well, Finn's behavior has been about the same. There has been no improvement for sure. He is still late all the time, and he still leaves the office a lot. I'm too busy to keep tabs on him or keep questioning him. I just hope this situation is resolved quickly so he can get back to doing his job. I'm getting tired of doing my job and his job."

Griffin sounded empathetic, "I'm sorry, Delaney. It's not fair to you, but I feel like our hands are tied. The sheriff doesn't want us to say anything to Finn. Please try to hang in there."

They disconnected the call. Delaney sat for a moment wondering what was happening with Finn. She prayed for him silently for a few moments. After the prayer, she realized she still had a lot of things left on her schedule. "I've got to get going." She cleared her desk off and headed over to labor and delivery to see Savannah.

Delaney reviewed Savannah's repeated labs, and then, she walked into Savannah's room after knocking. "Hey, lady, are you all tucked in here?" she asked.

Savannah replied, "You didn't warn me about that shot in my butt. It really hurt, and I heard I get another one tomorrow."

Delaney gave her an empathetic look, "I'm sorry. Those shots do hurt. You only have to get two. It would help if you had a little more meat on your bottom, you skinny thing."

Savannah chuckled. Delaney realized how good it was to see Savannah smiling. "So how is the adoption process going?"

Savannah hesitated, "Well, I think I've made up my mind."

Delaney raised her eyebrows and smiled, "That's great news. What have you decided?"

Savannah hesitated again and looked down at the floor.

Delaney walked over and sat down on the bed beside her. "Is everything okay? Are you thinking you want to keep her?"

"Oh no," said Savannah. "There is no way I can care for another child."

"Okay," said Delaney "So are you just struggling a little because you've finally chosen the adoptive parents?"

"No, not at all," Savannah replied. She added, "I feel at peace about my decision."

"Great," said Delaney with a wide smile. "So then what's wrong? You seem anxious."

Savannah looked up at her and stared at her for a moment. Then, she said, "Dr. Bartlett, I want you to adopt her."

Chapter 17

Delaney just stared at Savannah. Her heart was racing, and she started feeling short of breath. That statement was not quite what she had expected, not even close. Delaney was sure Savannah would have picked out an adoptive couple. Why would she choose her over an adoptive couple? It didn't make sense. Delaney shook her head and blinked as if she hadn't heard Savannah right, "Wait, what?"

"Dr. Bartlett, you have taken such good care of me and my baby. You are the reason I chose not to have an abortion. You said that you are almost forty, and you may not be able to have kids."

Delaney interrupted, "Yes, I did say that Savannah, but you shouldn't feel obligated to me at all."

Savannah smiled at her. "I don't feel obligated. I can't imagine my baby being raised by anyone else. You were meant to be her mom. I just know it. God put you in my life at this time so I could give my baby to you. I know that I will never have to worry about her. You have already shown me and her how much you care about us. I know you will love her like I do."

Delaney's mouth gaped open, and she was speechless. All she could say was, "Okay ... okay." She was still holding her breath.

Savannah eyed Delaney for a moment and then gave her a look of concern.

Delaney sensed the change and said, "Are you sure about this?"

Savannah said, "Yes, I'm sure, but are you okay with adopting a mixed baby?"

"What?" Delaney asked in a daze.

"My boyfriend is black, and I'm white. So she will be a mixed baby. Is that okay with you?" Savannah asked.

Delaney raised an eyebrow and rubbed her forehead. She smiled and said, "Of course, it is. I could love any child of any color, the way God loves each of us."

"I knew you would say that, Dr. Bartlett," Savannah replied with a wide smile. Then, she added, "So will you adopt her?"

Delaney looked straight at Savannah not knowing how she would manage a baby but exhaled and said with resolution, "Yes, I would love to."

Tears streamed down Savannah's face. "You can't imagine how happy this makes me," she said. She reached for Delaney, and Delaney leaned forward to hug her.

Delaney could feel fear and elation at the same time, as she hugged Savannah.

Savannah said, "I know you have to get a lawyer and some other stuff, but both me and my boyfriend will sign whatever papers we need to sign. We both agree that this is what we want."

Delaney nodded slowly, still feeling shocked. "I will get to work on that right away," she replied. She did her best to disguise her emotions, as she walked to the door. With her hand on the door knob, she said, "See you tomorrow, Savannah." Then, she turned to look at Savannah and said in a low and serious voice, "It takes a lot of courage to do what you're doing."

Savannah smiled with a face still wet from tears, "Thank you so much, Dr. Bartlett. This means so much to me."

Delaney smiled and nodded and then waved goodbye. On the drive home, her thoughts raced. Her heart felt heavy, but not bad. It felt full. She had adopted a baby. Was this real? Was she worthy to be a mom? Did she know how to be a mom? Could she do this alone? Savannah seemed to be so sure of her decision. How could she be so sure? "Lord, is this really what you want for me?" She prayed.

As Delaney turned and drove over the Lake Guntersville Bridge, snow started to fall. Big, fluffy flakes were falling on the windshield and all around her. By the time she reached her driveway, there was an inch of accumulated snow on the ground, and it continued to come down.

Delaney stepped out of her car onto the driveway and looked into the sky with wonder. The cold flakes melted on her face as she raised her eyes to the sky. It was beautiful, and a wave of peace came over her heart. She felt as if God's grace was pouring down on her. She had spent years tormented over her decision to abort. She had beaten herself down repeatedly for making that choice that felt unforgivable. There had been so much shame, and there still was, but today, she felt God's arms wrap around her when Savannah asked her to adopt her baby. The white snow gave her a feeling of cleansing, as if God was saying, "I love you, and I forgive you." Tears of joy and gratefulness flooded her eyes and ran down her face and onto the snow.

"Thank you for a second chance," she said, as she walked up and down her street taking in the beauty of the white, powdery precipitation. The snow was sticking to everything. She couldn't believe it. She had been told there wouldn't be snow in Guntersville or maybe only a dusting at most. All along her street, her neighbors had stepped outside to delight in the glistening beauty of the falling flakes.

Delaney started to feel chilled and decided to go inside. Inside the foyer, she closed the door and took off her coat. She stepped up to the window and leaned on it. It was almost dark now, and the snow continued to fall gracefully from the heavens. Delaney now understood that God wanted her to adopt this baby, despite all the fears that had jabbed at her heart. Since her abortion, she had been unable to feel worthy of a child. Today, God had spoken to her heart. He had wrapped His loving arms around her and given her His peace. She finally understood that He had forgiven her and that she needed to forgive herself.

Delaney awoke the next morning and slowly rolled out of bed. Once she was awake, her first thought was of Savannah and the baby. A wave of excitement and panic washed over her at the same time. She smiled as the reality of the adoption was sinking in, but she knew she had some work to do to get ready for the baby. She called an attorney to put the legal paperwork in motion. The attorney discussed the adoption process with her and scheduled a home study for the next day. He was going to meet with Savannah and her boyfriend to have them sign the paperwork, and then, he would have Delaney sign her part. Delaney couldn't believe how straightforward the process seemed. She had heard other adoption stories, and so far, this adoption story was nothing like those.

She realized that she had less than eight weeks to prepare for a baby in her home and in her life. She wanted to call someone to share her exciting news. But who could she call? She still had fears, lots of them. What if the adoption isn't actually straightforward? What will people think of this adoption? How will I care for this baby and be a mom with my full-time job? What if I allow myself to bond with the baby, and then, Savannah changes her mind at the last minute? How can I be a good mommy without a daddy for her? Delaney started to feel overwhelmed. Despite God's peace from the night before, her human heart still felt fearful. But at the same time, she felt a sense of coming joy. She wished she could call her mom and dad.

She exhaled as she thought of Ben. She wanted to call him and share her good news, but she knew she couldn't. He might not feel excited for her because of his own loss, and it might be more like adding salt to an open wound for him. He had also been distant since Christmas Eve. He had hardly looked at her or spoken to her at the hospital. She felt as if she had done something to make him be so distant, but she couldn't come up with anything. The few times she had tried to spark a conversation, he seemed busy or about to leave. He had seemed to care for her at one time, but since Christmas Eve, there was no sign of any emotion from him. He had become the stoic, sad Ben she had first met.

Chapter 18

❦❦❦❦❦❦

The next day, as Delaney arrived at labor and delivery, Krissy was sitting at the desk. "Hi, Dr. B," she said.

"Good morning, Krissy. How are you today?" Delaney answered.

Krissy was grinning from ear to ear. "I heard your exciting news. Savannah told me."

Delaney took a double take at her as she set her purse down. "Oh really?"

"Why didn't you call me and tell me about the adoption?" Krissy inquired, looking injured.

"I barely just found out myself," replied Delaney. "It still hasn't sunk in. Besides, Savannah might change her mind, and I'm okay with that. I have to keep my heart at a safe distance right now."

Krissy shook her head. "You really don't get it, do you?"

Delaney looked at her with a blank stare. "What?"

Krissy said, "This young lady feels so relieved and at peace to know that such a caring woman and doctor is going to love her child and provide for her. She can't care for this baby like you can. She is a young mother who loves her child so much that she knows her child belongs with you. She's not looking back. You are this baby's mother for the rest of her life."

Delaney sat down. She had to let Krissy's words sink in. If Krissy was right, then Delaney knew she was not ready. "Help me get ready for this baby, please. I don't know what I need."

Krissy replied with an official motherhood answer, "I would be glad to help you prepare for your daughter's arrival. It's an honor, and I can't tell you how happy I am for you. What a blessing for you."

At that, Krissy pulled out a blank piece of paper and started making a list. Delaney leaned over her shoulder as she wrote.

"You'll need a crib with sheets, blankets, a changing table, car seat, rocking chair, baby bathtub, bottles, sterilizer, pacifiers, lots of diapers." As Krissy read the list, she was interrupted.

"Hey, ladies," said Ben as he came down the hall toward the desk. Both ladies looked up and acknowledged him. Delaney felt her heart jump into her throat at the sight of him. "Here are the instruments you asked for, Krissy," he said.

"You're an angel, Ben. Thank you. Someone else we know is having an angel soon," said Krissy.

Ben tilted his head with a look of confusion and asked, "What?"

Krissy looked at Delaney.

Delaney hesitated, but then said, "I'm having a baby."

Ben's face turned white, and he expressed a look of shock. He stammered, "Oh … okay, wow. Congratulations, then. When will the baby be here?"

Delaney shook her head as she corrected her statement, "I mean, I'm adopting a baby."

Ben appeared to exhale. His thoughts raced at the idea of Delaney being pregnant. He had never thought about that happening, but why would it bother him so much? He could feel jealousy and nausea creeping in at the thought of her with another man. He shouldn't be thinking that way, but he was.

"Yesterday," said Krissy.

"It's kind of a long and unusual story," added Delaney.

"I've got time to hear it," Ben replied.

Delaney told him the story of Savannah and how she had shown up late for prenatal care and had the dilemma of caring for another child without the help of the father of the baby. She relayed the story of Savannah's search for an adoptive family, but not being able to find peace with her decision. "She asked me to adopt her, and I agreed. It was pretty simple. I told her it could be an open adoption too." Delaney decided not to say anything to anyone about Savannah's early thoughts on aborting the baby. It really wasn't anyone's business anyway.

"I'm sure you've already thought about this, but are you hiring a nanny or babysitter to stay with her since you work so much?" Ben asked. Then, he added, "Knowing how big your heart is, you'll probably have trouble letting go of her every day when you leave for work. You will find it hard to go one moment without her once you are her mom." With that comment, his face became overwhelmed with sadness, and his affect changed, as Delaney had seen it do many times before. He could go from happy and relaxed to sad and strained at the snap of a finger. He looked down at the ground uncomfortably and said, "I need to get going. Good luck with the baby, Dr. Bartlett. I'm sure everything will work out. Congratulations, again."

Delaney felt his sadness as he walked away. She knew he was hurting and missing his daughter. It had to be hard for him to hear about her adoption. She only wished she could wrap her arms around him and comfort him.

"He's such a hottie, Dr. B," said Krissy. "You really need to think about dating him."

"I think he has his heart full of sad memories right now, and I have my hands full with a new baby coming. Let's get back to this list. I'm going to have to order most of this online," Delaney said. "And Ben is right, how will I take care of her with the way I work?"

"You'll figure it out. All right, let's get back to the baby details, but don't go dismissing Ben just yet, okay? I really think the two of you would be great together."

Delaney nodded to satisfy Krissy's request, but she knew she would have no such future with the gorgeous man. He was already taken by memories and would be forever.

Delaney returned home after discharging Savannah from the hospital. The baby was due in only eight weeks. She had a lot to do. She sat down at her desk and proceeded to search for and order the online items she needed. Next, she touched base with her attorney to make sure the adoption paperwork was moving forward. The last thing she did was to call a colleague at the St. Jo's Medical Center South hospital in the close by town of Boaz. She realized that it would be a conflict of interest to deliver the baby, so she transferred Savannah's care to her colleague there. Dr. Jamison would deliver the baby.

As for childcare, she guessed that Ben was right. She hadn't even met the sweet baby, but she already knew that being separated from her would be hard. She considered hiring a nanny, since that would make the most sense. However, she could already feel the tug at her heart if she would have to leave her every day. Maybe she would at least start by setting up a nursery in her office. That could definitely work in the short term.

Chapter 19

It was the first Saturday in February, and Savannah was now thirty-six weeks. Her platelets were still low, but they were stable. Dr. Jamison was checking them twice a week now. He was aware from her previous two pregnancies that her platelets could get low quickly. If they dropped below fifty, he would deliver her. Delaney sat on pins and needles as she waited to hear from Savannah after each of her appointments with Dr. Jamison, knowing that he could choose to deliver her at any time.

The nursery at home and at work were both set up and ready to go. Delaney was on call, but the hospital was quiet, so she was at home. The house was clean, and the laundry was done. Delaney paced around the house feeling apprehensive. Finally, she walked into the nursery and sat in the rocking chair. She couldn't believe that a little baby would soon live in this room and that she would be her mommy. She prayed, "Lord, I trust you with this adoption. Please let your will be done, and please help me to be a good mom. Show me how to juggle all of this responsibility. I know you'll help me find a way. Please give Savannah strength as she courageously gives up her baby for adoption."

Delaney stood up and walked over to the dresser she had bought. She reached into the first drawer and pulled out one of the tiny dresses for the baby. She marveled at the miniature size and the wonder of human life. She still wondered why God would entrust her with this little one, even after she had aborted her own baby years ago. She tried to submerge that thought. In her heart, she knew God had forgiven her, but would she ever be able to forgive herself? She was thankful when her cell phone rang.

"Hello?"

"Hey, Dr. Bartlett. This is Griffin. Did I catch you at an okay time?" he asked.

"Yes, of course," she answered with furrowed eyebrows. Why was Griffin calling her on a Saturday? She continued, "Things are relatively quiet right now, so I'm at home. How can I help?"

"Well, I don't know how to tell you this news without just saying it," he said.

Delaney could feel her heart start pounding. What could it be? She didn't speak.

Griffin went on, "Finn has been arrested."

Delaney's eyes widened as if they were bugging out, and her mouth gaped open. She stood from the rocking chair and continued standing, frozen and dumbfounded. Finally, she found her voice and exclaimed, "What happened?"

"He's been arrested for a DUI. He's in jail and will have a court date in a week or so, but he won't be coming back to work any time soon," he said.

"I … I'm shocked. I don't even know what to say," she said.

He replied, "I know. Me too." He hesitated and then said, "I talked to him today, and he confessed to me that he's been drinking a lot, every day, and almost all day. That Red Bull can he was always drinking from, well, let's just say, it wasn't Red Bull." Griffin paused for a few moments. Then, he continued, "It explains his behavior as of late. He said he's not been able to deal with the divorce and losing his wife. He admits he has a problem with alcohol, and he wants help. I feel sorry for him. He's got a nasty court battle ahead of him, and then, he'll go into rehabilitation. I hope he gets the help he needs."

Delaney suddenly realized that Finn would no longer be her partner at the practice. He was going to be out for a long time, probably months to years. Her voice cracked as she asked, "Griffin, how am I going to take on his patients on top of my patients and care for a newborn baby? You know I'm adopting a baby, right?"

"Yes, I heard that, and congratulations. I'm sorry to give you this bad news when something so good is happening in your life. Let me work on getting some temporary call coverage for you. I promise

I'll do my best. I'm sorry this mess has been dumped on you. On top of everything else, the DEA is involved."

"What? Why?" Delaney's pulse started to race again.

Griffin replied, "They think he may have been selling narcotics to buy his wife more drugs. They didn't say for sure, but it sounds like he spent a lot of money pretty quickly. The DEA will probably question you on Monday. They will be in Finn's office all day going through his things."

Delaney exhaled loudly trying to take in every word Griffin spoke. It was overwhelming. After sitting silently for a few moments, she said, "Okay. I'll do whatever I need to do, which means I'll help the DEA however I can. I'll just believe that all of this is going to work out somehow."

"Thanks for your cooperation and hard work. The hospital will be paying you for the extra call coverage," said Griffin. There was a pause and then he added, "I hope the extra income helps to cushion this blow a little. I'm already working on finding another doctor to help, but right now, I can't promise you I can get help right away."

Delaney closed her eyes. She knew he was telling her that she might have to endure coverage for 24-7 for a while. This did not sit well with her, given the fact that the baby would be here soon. "Well," she said, "at least the baby won't be delivered for three weeks. Hopefully, that will be enough time to find a doctor to help cover the call. Thanks for everything you're doing, Griffin."

They disconnected the call, and Delaney sat back down in the rocking chair. She stared at the ceiling for a while trying to process the news about Finn. She couldn't believe he was in this much trouble. He had lied to everyone, especially to her. They were old friends, and this made her mad. But mostly, it made her sad.

Chapter 20

On Monday morning, as Delaney pulled into the parking lot, the press was waiting outside the office. Griffin had anticipated their interest and greeted them at the door. He made himself available to do interviews with both the local newspaper and local TV station. Thankfully, they went away after that. Delaney was grateful that he had intercepted them so she didn't have to comment. The DEA showed up at nine o'clock and set up camp in Finn's office. The office door remained mostly closed throughout their investigation that morning. Detective Brady was the lead detective on the case and was expected to interview Delaney and the rest of the office staff.

"Dr. Bartlett?" interrupted Detective Brady, as Delaney was eating her lunch at her desk.

Delaney looked up from the chart she was reviewing, "Yes?"

"I know we've already been introduced, but I'm Detective Brady. Do you have a few minutes to answer some questions?" Detective Brady was a tall man with broad shoulders and a head of dark brown hair, cut in a crew cut. He was wearing a black T-shirt, black parachute pants, and black boots. He had a gun in a holster at his waist. He had a kind face, but his eyes were serious and intimidating. He looked like a sniper from a few of the movies she'd seen in the past. All he needed was black paint on his face.

"Of course," she said, standing up.

"Would you follow me, please?" he asked.

Delaney followed him into the office conference room. There were two other agents sitting at the table. She assumed they were DEA agents, because they were all dressed the same way and had the same matter-of-fact looks on their faces. The two agents looked up without saying anything, as Delaney walked into the room. Detective Brady motioned for her to sit in a chair at the table, and then, he leaned on the table in front of her. He looked up at another agent standing at the door and nodded. The agent closed the door. He looked back at Delaney and then looked across the table at the other two agents.

"Let's get started," he said still looking at them. One of them had a notepad and pen and looked ready to take notes. The other one was holding what looked like a high-tech voice recorder. He nodded at both of them and then turned his attention to Delaney. "Now, Dr. Bartlett, I'm going to ask you a series of questions. Just answer them as honestly as you can."

Delaney nodded as she felt perspiration forming on her upper lip. She was nervous, though she knew she didn't have anything to be nervous about. She had never come this close to any part of the law before now, except for a couple of speeding tickets. This process was intimidating, and she felt the need to answer honestly and quickly so she could get out of there.

"Dr. Bartlett, what is your relationship with Finn Donovan?" he started.

Delaney answered, "Finn is a good friend and colleague. We did our training together at the University of Louisville in Kentucky."

"Did you know Finn had an alcohol abuse problem?" he asked, staring at her with an intensity that was almost painful.

"No, I had no idea. I mean, I've had a cocktail with him before, but I've never seen him drunk or act unruly," she replied.

"Did you know he was going through a divorce?" he asked.

"Yes, I confronted him a few weeks ago about his behavior at work. Griffin had received complaints, and I had noticed some things at work too. I asked him what was going on, and he told me his wife had an opiate addiction and that she was leaving him," she said. Her throat was dry, and the air in the room became stuffy.

"What kind of behaviors are you talking about?" he asked.

Delaney looked over at the two agents. The one was furiously writing notes, while the other one was tweaking the knobs on the high-tech voice recorder. Delaney looked back at Detective Brady and said, "Well, he started getting behind on his medical records. He was showing up late for scheduled surgeries to the point that he lost his surgery block time. He wasn't answering his phone on call and was missing deliveries. He would sometimes leave the office in the middle of the day for an hour or two. No one knew where he went. Then, the sheriff showed up last week to talk to him."

Detective Brady took a deep breath and sat in silence for a moment. "Dr. Bartlett, do you have any knowledge of Finn selling narcotic prescriptions for cash?"

Delaney felt like she was on the witness stand. Her heart was racing as she could feel the heaviness of his glare at her. She looked directly in his eyes and said, "Detective Brady, until last Saturday, I did not. The first time I heard that he might be selling prescription narcotics for money was from Griffin on Saturday. Griffin only mentioned it to me after he found out the DEA suspected it. I'm appalled by the news, and I hope it's not true."

Detective Brady gave her a half smile, as if he was trying to intimidate some information out of her. He leaned in closer to her and asked, "Would you ever sell narcotic prescriptions for money?"

Delaney exhaled loudly and furrowed her brow. She wanted to punch him. He was insulting her on purpose, and she knew it. She had done a few depositions in residency training, and she knew he was baiting her for a reaction, just like the lawyers had done during those depositions. She didn't bite. Instead, she calmly replied, "Of course not. It's illegal and unethical. I choose to do the right thing at all times, especially when it comes to the seriousness of my role as a doctor."

Detective Brady crossed his arms on his chest and was still leaning on the table with his feet crossed. "Well," he paused. "Did you know Finn was selling narcotic prescriptions for money in order to buy drugs for himself?"

Delaney was shocked, and it showed on her face. She hesitated and then said "No," with disbelief in her voice. Then, she asked, "Was he really?"

Detective Brady didn't answer her. He stood up and nodded to the agent at the door to open the door. "You can go now, Dr. Bartlett.

Thank you for your cooperation. We will be in touch if we have any further questions."

Delaney was puzzled. She figured he would have had many more questions, but she was glad that he didn't. He dismissed her, and she was thrilled to breathe fresh air from the hallway. She returned to her office and plopped down in her chair. What had Finn done? Did he really have a drug addiction too? How could he be so reckless with his privileges as a doctor and abuse his ability to write prescriptions? She wasn't sure if it was all true. Detective Brady had tried to be intimidating. Maybe he had embellished the facts to see if Delaney would corroborate his suspicions. She didn't know, and at this point, she didn't want to know. She just wanted to finish seeing afternoon patients and go home.

Chapter 21

Thursday afternoon of that week, Delaney was delighted to see the DEA agents pack up their investigation and leave. All week, their presence had weighed heavily on her and her office staff. Everyone was ready to get back to some kind of normalcy, though they were still far from that. Delaney felt as if she'd been doing damage control all week, as she'd had to see all of Finn's patients. Since the case had gone public on the news, Finn's patients wanted answers about their care. They wanted Delaney to review their records to be sure Finn had provided appropriate treatments. Wanting to calm their fears, Delaney had to spend extra time with his patients, and she was exhausted.

As 6:00 p.m. rolled around, Delaney finished up a few more patient visits and then sat in her office to do some paperwork. Her cell phone chimed with an unknown, incoming call.

"Hello?"

"Dr. Bartlett?"

"Yes."

"Hey, it's Todd Jamison. I'm taking care of Savannah Carter," he reminded her.

"Yes, of course," she replied. "What's going on?" She asked feeling a sudden jolt of worry.

"Well, it's time to have a baby," he started. Then, he added, "Her platelets are down to fifty."

Delaney held her breath. "Is Savannah there? Does the baby look okay?" She asked feeling her stomach jump into her throat.

"Yeah, I put her in the hospital earlier today, and the baby's heart rate has looked fine on the monitors. I'm glad you gave her a course of steroids earlier in the pregnancy, since she's only a little over thirty-seven weeks. The C-section is at seven thirty tonight," he said.

Delaney tried to sound professional, though inside she felt a flurry of worry and excitement. She replied, "Okay great, Todd. Thank you for letting me know. I'll come down to the south hospital now. I'm leaving the office."

After they disconnected, she called Labor and Delivery. She was glad when Krissy answered.

"Krissy, it's Delaney. Savannah is having her baby tonight at seven thirty. I'm a nervous wreck. What do I do? Is there anything going on over there? Are there any triage patients? I have to drive to the south hospital, and it's thirty minutes away." Delaney hardly breathed while she rattled off the information and questions.

"Slow down," said Krissy. "You're going to be a mom. You're not conquering the world. Breathe," she added.

Delaney exhaled, "Yes, okay. You're right. I'm just worried that I will get there, and then, I'll have to leave to do a delivery or surgery here. Plus, I'm just nervous because the baby will actually be here tonight."

"I know," said Krissy. "But everything is going to be okay. I'm so excited she'll be here tonight. I will call you if there is any hint of a patient showing up here. We can triage from here, and it will work out. Don't worry. Go be with your daughter."

"Thanks, Krissy. Thanks for being here for me," said Delaney. She disconnected the call, called her attorney, and asked him to send the adoption paperwork to the hospital and then drove straight to the hospital. Upon her arrival, Savannah had already been taken back to the operating room. Delaney was upset that she hadn't been able to see her before the surgery. The nurses directed her to the waiting room after they placed a baby band on her wrist. Savannah had instructed the nurses to put the baby band on Delaney's wrist instead of her own. This was the band that identified the baby's mother. All of the adoption paperwork had gone through, and Delaney was being recognized as the baby's mother.

Delaney stared at the band. It said "Baby Girl Carter." She was really about to become a mommy. Her heart raced, as she fought back all of the fears she had about the adoption, about being a mom, and about how she would be able to manage so many changes in her life. For a moment, Ben's face flashed in her mind. Oh how she could use his strong shoulder to lean on. She silently prayed for Savannah and for strength.

The surgery took longer than Delaney thought it should, and she started to worry. After a little more time passed, one of the nurses came to the waiting room and introduced herself as Pepper. She asked Delaney to follow her through the double doors into the nursery.

As Delaney followed her, Pepper said, "Dr. Jamison said the surgery was not easy. He said Savannah had a lot of scar tissue, and it took him awhile to get the baby out. He is just finishing up the closure now, but you can come see the baby."

Delaney felt a lump form in her throat. "Okay, well, is the baby okay? Is Savannah okay?"

As they entered the nursery, there was only one baby there. Delaney knew this was her baby, but what she saw made her walk faster to the baby's bedside. As she approached the baby, she could see that an oxygen hood had been placed over her. Delaney knew this meant that she was having trouble breathing. A tiny IV had been started in her little arm, and it was protected by a gauze wrap to keep it in place.

Pepper looked at Delaney's worried face and said, "I think she's just having some transitional respiratory distress. I think it will get better. The pediatrician, Dr. Jonah, is on his way in to evaluate her. Try not to worry."

Delaney stared at the sweet little baby with a head full of dark curly hair. Her skin was light, and she was wrinkled and beautiful. Delaney knew enough about newborns to know her color wasn't a healthy pink, and she wasn't crying or moving as much as a healthy newborn should. She reached for the baby's little hand. The baby wrapped her fingers around Delaney's index finger with a tight hold. Delaney's breath caught in her throat as she held back tears. She fought to maintain her strength, and she prayed. As the little fingers held onto her finger, the baby appeared to turn pink and started crying and kicking.

"Well, she's started to act like a grown up now, kicking and screaming," said Dr. Jonah as he arrived at the bedside with a big grin. He looked at Delaney. "Hi, are you Dr. Bartlett, the adoptive mom?"

She smiled at him and said, "Yes. Please call me Delaney." Delaney stepped aside to let Dr. Jonah examine the baby.

"I think she's going to be just fine, but we will leave her under the oxyhood for tonight. I'm sorry you can't hold her yet," he said pursing his lips.

"That's okay," she replied. "I'm just glad she's going to be okay." Delaney felt a wave of relief come over her heart and body. She turned to Pepper and asked, "Is Savannah okay?"

Pepper replied, "Yes, she's in recovery still waking up. You can see her if you'd like."

"Hey, Delaney," said Dr. Jamison, walking into the nursery. He still had his surgery hat on. "I just had a little trouble getting down to the uterus because of scar tissue. So the surgery took a little longer than I thought it would. Savannah is doing fine, though. It all went well."

Delaney shook his hand and then hugged him. "Thank you so much. This whole situation is so emotionally charged for me."

"I can only imagine," he replied. Then, he added, "I heard what happened with Finn. That situation was dumped on you. I'm so sorry to hear about your dilemma. I can't imagine taking call by myself all the time. They're going to get you some help, right?"

Delaney sighed and shook her head, "I hope so, because I've got a lot on my plate." She stared at the little baby, who was now wriggling around and having fits of cute attitude. She cried out and seemed to be yelling at Dr. Jonah for messing with her. Delaney looked back toward Dr. Jamison and said, "They are going to keep her under the oxyhood tonight, but they think she will transition just fine."

"That's great. She's beautiful. Congratulations." He shook her hand again and then left to check on Savannah.

Delaney couldn't take her eyes off the sweet, crying, baby girl. The whole thing seemed surreal. This little baby was her baby. She told herself this over and over, but it wouldn't sink in. She knew she was holding back and protecting herself, in case Savannah changed her mind.

Delaney's cell phone rang, and she pulled it from her purse to answer it.

"Dr. Bartlett, is she here? Is that her that I hear crying?" Krissy asked with excitement.

"Yes, she's here. She's beautiful." Delaney replied.

"How much does she weigh?" asked Krissy.

Delaney looked at the baby information card on the baby's bed. It read "6 lbs 12 oz." She read the weight to Krissy.

"Awww, she's so small. Send me some pictures as soon as you can," she said.

"I will. Is everything okay there?" Delaney asked.

"Well, I wish I didn't have to tell you this, but we have a full-term patient here. Her water broke at 8:00 p.m., and she is scheduled for a repeat C-section. She's was one of Dr. Donovan's patients." Krissy added, "I'm so sorry."

"It's fine, Krissy. I have to do what I have to do. Can you get her ready for surgery? I will head that way in a minute. The baby has to stay under the oxyhood tonight anyway, so I can't hold her." Delaney frowned knowing that she had to leave the baby for a few hours. Ben had been right. She was already feeling that mommy tug on her heart. She didn't want to be separated from her, not even for a minute.

On her way out, Delaney stopped in to check on Savannah. She was reclining in the hospital bed eating ice chips. She was groggy from the anesthesia and still in a lot of pain. Delaney leaned in and kissed her forehead. "She's really beautiful and perfect," Delaney said.

Savannah smiled and replied, "I'm so glad you like her. You are her momma."

At that, Delaney just nodded. Savannah hadn't seen her yet. Delaney feared that Savannah would probably not be able to give her up. Delaney took a deep breath and told herself it was okay, though. She believed God had a plan, and she had decided to trust Him. "I have to go do a C-section," Delaney said in a quiet voice. "I'll come check on you tomorrow. I'm so proud of you."

Savannah smiled but then furrowed her brow. "You need to stay and hold your baby."

Delaney explained how the baby needed to stay under the oxyhood overnight. Savannah seemed okay with the explanation. Savannah started to drift off, so Delaney took the cup of ice from her and set it on the bedside table.

She turned to walk out of the room when she heard Savannah ask, "What did you name her?"

Delaney turned to face Savannah. Her eyes were open, and she stared at Delaney. Delaney hadn't thought about a name. She had been so overwhelmed by so many other things that naming the baby had been bumped down on her list. If she had to be honest, though, she wasn't ready to name a baby that might not come home with her. "I don't know yet. I wanted to see her first," Delaney replied.

"Please give her a strong name that has a special meaning," she said.

Delaney smiled and replied, "I can't imagine any other kind of name. I promise I will. Good night and see you tomorrow."

Chapter 22

D elaney was finished with the C-section and ready to leave the hospital by midnight. She called Pepper to check on the baby, and Pepper told her she was doing well and would be on room air by mid-morning. Delaney wanted to go back to be with the baby, but Pepper told her to go home and rest. She said that the baby couldn't be held until she was out of the oxyhood, so Delaney complied and reluctantly drove home.

It was late, but she couldn't sleep. She needed to pick out a name for the baby and thought about what Savannah had asked of her earlier. At home, she sat down at her desk and began to browse baby names online. The endless lists of names quickly became overwhelming. She decided to take a different approach, so she made a list of meanings she wanted the name to have. For Delaney, the baby was a gift of grace from God. "Grace" was the perfect first name. She also wanted her name to show dedication to God. She searched for a middle name and finally came up with "Elyse," which meant "consecrated to God." She put the two names together a few different ways, and then, she sat back and smiled. "This is it, Lord," she said out loud. "Gracie Elyse." She laid her pen down and stared at the name. She was sure Savannah would approve.

It was after midnight, and Delaney's eyelids were growing heavy. She realized she had better try to sleep while she could, because she might be called in for another patient. She wanted to spend the rest of her time that day with Gracie and would head out to the hospital in only a few hours. She prayed that she would not get called in for a delivery or surgery.

After a few hours of rest, Delaney poured a cup of coffee into her travel mug and headed out. She arrived on Labor and Delivery at the south hospital at 7:00 a.m. that morning. Pepper was getting ready to leave, since her shift was over.

"Good morning, Dr. Bartlett. She did great last night," Pepper said. She held up her index finger. "Hold on," she added, as she disappeared into the nursery and returned with Gracie in her arms. She was still sleeping and wrapped snugly in a baby blanket. Pepper handed the little bundle to Delaney.

Delaney's heart felt light and full at the same time. "Thank you," she said. She peered down into the little face and studied her tiny features. She was so precious. Delaney fought back the lump in her throat, but she couldn't stop the tears from forming.

Pepper said, "Savannah fed her and changed her diaper about thirty minutes ago. She shouldn't need to eat for another two hours."

Delaney looked up at Pepper after hearing this news. She felt a wave of anxiety. "Did Savannah do okay with that?"

"Yes, she really seems to be at peace. She wanted to see her and hold her just one time," Pepper replied.

"I completely understand," Delaney replied.

"We've set up one of the rooms so you can stay with the baby. Have you named her yet?" Pepper asked. "We need to start working on her birth certificate."

"Okay, thanks. Yes, her name is Gracie Elyse," Delaney replied.

"It's a beautiful name," said Pepper. "Come with me, and I'll show you your room."

Delaney followed Pepper to a room at the end of the hall. Pepper did the required new mommy teaching with Delaney. Delaney was attentive as the two women discussed formula feeding, diaper changes, the umbilical stump care, choking precautions, and sleeping precautions. Pepper gave Delaney a piece of paper with a chart on it and asked Delaney to record the amount of formula Gracie drank and how many wet or dirty diapers she had. "I'll be back for the night shift tonight, so I'll see you then. Have a wonderful day with Gracie."

"Thank you," she replied with a smile. "Oh, Pepper, can I see Savannah today?" She asked as Pepper was leaving.

"Of course. If, at any time, you need to step out or leave, just bring Gracie to the nurse's desk, and we will babysit her," Pepper said. Then she added, "Oh, also, Dr. Jonah will be in to examine her this morning, so we'll be coming to take her to the nursery for an hour or so."

Delaney nodded, and Pepper left. Delaney sat on the hospital bed holding Gracie to her chest. She slept so peacefully. Delaney could feel the fast rise and fall of her little chest with every breath. Delaney's heart felt full to the point of overflowing. She kissed her little, soft head of hair. She felt so perfect in Delaney's arms. "I'm a mommy," she whispered. "Thank you, Father," she whispered again looking out the window with tears glistening in her eyes.

Daylight was starting to cast its light, and Delaney did a double take as she thought she saw snowflakes. She walked over to the window with Gracie in her arms and stared outside for a few moments. Sure enough, it was snowing. A second snow fall in Alabama seemed unlikely, but there it was. Delaney breathed out slowly and smiled. She felt a deep sense of peace as she watched the flakes floating to the ground. In the quiet of the room, holding this precious gift to her chest, she felt the weight of God's message to her again. He was reminding her that she was forgiven, that she was worthy, and that He was pouring His grace out on her.

Delaney walked over to the bed. She took her shoes off and climbed onto the bed gently without waking Gracie. She perched herself up against a couple of pillows and, in the quiet, surveyed the room. She looked at the empty couch beside the bed. Just like at her hospital, this was the couch for the father of the baby. Her heart ached just a little as she wished for that feeling of a complete family. Then, she stopped herself and, instead, thanked God for the miracles He had worked in her life. "Thank you for Gracie, Lord. My heart is overflowing. I'm so blessed," she whispered.

Delaney heard a knock on the door. She looked up and was surprised to see Savannah open the door and peek through.

"Hi, can I come in for a minute?" she asked.

"Hi, Savannah, of course. Please come in and sit with us," Delaney replied.

Savannah walked with slow, careful steps to the couch and sat down. She folded her hands in front of her without saying anything.

Delaney felt anxiety creeping in. This was the moment she had dreaded. She was sure Savannah would tell her she was doubting her decision to adopt out the baby.

"Do you want to hold her?" Delaney asked, leaning forward.

"No, I held her this morning. I wanted to feed her and change her diaper just once. I talked to her and explained to her why you are her mommy. I know she understands," Savannah replied. "I came in here to tell you not to worry about me changing my mind. As hard as it is for me to give her up, I feel stronger about knowing you are going to love her and care for her. You can provide her with everything she needs."

Delaney exhaled, "Thank you, Savannah. I already love her so much. She is perfect."

"Have you thought of a name? Because if you haven't, I thought you might want to consider 'Grace,' because God has been graceful to me through this situation. But you don't have to pick that name, I …" Savannah started to say.

Delaney interrupted, "Her name is Gracie Elyse."

Savannah grinned from ear to ear, and her eyes filled with tears. "Thank you, I love it. It's perfect." She stared at the baby for a few more moments and then stood up. "I'm going to go back to bed. I'm pretty sore. If it's okay with you, I'd rather not see Gracie for several months. Although I'm at peace with my decision, I need some time and space, if you know what I mean. But I hope you will text me plenty of pictures."

Delaney nodded with pursed lips.

"I also have a two-year-old at home who needs me. Please don't worry about me or me changing my mind about the adoption. I know you do. You have a big heart, and that's why I know you're the right mommy for her." Savannah leaned in and gave Delaney and Gracie a gentle, group hug and then went back to her room.

Chapter 23

Delaney enjoyed the rest of the day with Gracie, with the exception of the hour that Dr. Jonah took Gracie to examine her. During that time, she brought lunch to Savannah and sat with her. After that hour, she returned to Gracie. Delaney could see a routine already starting with Gracie's eating and sleeping schedule. She held her all day. She had heard some people say that holding a baby all the time would only spoil her, but Delaney didn't care. Gracie was an angel, and she loved her with her whole being and couldn't stand to be apart from her.

At 7:30 p.m., Pepper peeked in the room. "Hey there, I just came in at seven, and I wanted to check on you. How was your day?" she asked.

Delaney was sitting up in the bed with Gracie nestled to her chest. Gracie had just fallen asleep after being fed and burped. "We are doing great. We've had a wonderful day." Delaney's cell phone rang, and she answered it before it could ring a second time and wake up Gracie. Pepper stood quietly at the bedside.

"Hello?"

"Hey, Delaney. This is Doc in the ER."

"Oh, hi. What's up?" She asked feeling her heart sink into her gut.

Doc said, "Sorry to bother you, but I have a patient here with an ectopic pregnancy. She was one of Dr. Donovan's patients. Her name is Tara Smith. Ultrasound shows a right-sided pelvic mass and a quantitative pregnancy level of 5,200."

Delaney's face showed the disappointment she felt.

Pepper furrowed her brow in reaction to Delaney's face.

Delaney spoke into the phone, "Okay, would you please do me a favor and call Ben and ask him to call the surgery team in? I'm at the south hospital, and I'll head that way. I'll see the patient in the preoperative area to discuss the surgery with her."

"Sure thing," he said. Then, he asked, "What are you doing at the south hospital?"

Delaney pursed her lips and tried to smile, "My baby is here, the one I'm adopting. So I'm with her."

Doc replied, "That's awesome. Congratulations! I'm so sorry to drag you away from her. It really stinks that you don't have any coverage help right now."

Delaney replied, "It's okay. I'm just focusing on the positives. I feel blessed, and anyway, this surgery shouldn't take long."

They disconnected the call, and Delaney looked up at Pepper. "Can you please take her for a while? I have to go do surgery."

Pepper smiled, but also had a pained look on her face for Delaney, "Of course. Sorry you have to leave."

Delaney replied, "I'll be back after the surgery, probably by ten o'clock."

Pepper smiled bigger, "Sure, I'll take good care of her and have her ready for you when you get back."

Delaney kissed Gracie's cheek and begrudgingly handed Gracie to Pepper, "Thanks."

Delaney drove the thirty minutes to the north hospital. The surgical patient, Ms. Smith, had a pregnancy in one of her tubes, rather than in the uterus where it should be. In a matter of time, the pregnancy would outgrow the tube, and the tube would rupture and bleed, if it wasn't removed. This situation was considered an emergency.

In the hospital, Delaney walked directly to the preoperative area to see Ms. Smith. After Delaney did an examination and had a full discussion with Ms. Smith about the surgery, Ms. Smith commented, "I'm glad you're the one doing my surgery and not Dr. Donovan."

Delaney nodded without wanting to discuss Finn and said, "I'm glad I'm here, too."

Delaney changed into scrubs and sat in the lounge waiting for the surgery team to be ready. She felt her heart grow heavy, as she thought about Finn, her situation with the call coverage, and Gracie. Her thoughts were interrupted, as Ben walked into the lounge.

"Oh, hey, I didn't know you were in here. How are you?" he asked.

Delaney's heart jumped, and her pulse started to race at the sight of him. She'd been so busy with Finn's investigation and damage control, as well as preparing for Gracie, that she hadn't had time to think about him.

"Hi," she said.

"I heard you have a patient with an ectopic pregnancy to operate on," he said.

"Yes, it's pretty classic, but not ruptured yet. I want to use the laparoscope," she answered.

"Okay, I figured. I think we are ready to go if you are," he said.

"Yes, the sooner the better," she replied.

He stared at her for a moment as if debating whether or not he would ask the question on his mind. Then, he asked, "Do you have somewhere you need to be?"

Delaney took in a deep breath and then answered, "Yes, my daughter was born last night. I've been at the hospital all day with her, but I had to leave to come here. I'd like to get back to her."

Ben raised his eyebrows at the good news and smiled, "Oh, I hadn't heard. Congratulations. That's really great, Dr. Bartlett. I'm sorry you have to be here."

She shook her head, "It's okay. It is what it is. I'll just finish up here and get back to her."

Ben decided to maintain his distance and didn't ask any more questions. He just nodded and left the room. He called for Ms. Smith to be sent back to the OR and then sat back in his chair with his arms perched behind his head.

He missed Delaney. His heart had leapt when he saw her. He knew she was struggling right now with the turmoil Finn had caused. He felt empathy for her having to be pulled away from her brand-new baby. He just didn't know if he could bring himself to help her, to get involved. He cared for Delaney deeply, but he didn't know if he could find a way to care for her without feeling guilty.

After the surgery, Delaney started to get in her car to head back to Gracie. The baby car seat was sitting in a box in the back seat and caught her eye. It needed to be installed for tomorrow, because she was bringing Gracie home. She decided to go ahead and install it. This decision was an obvious miscalculation of her talents. She worked at it for over thirty minutes, but her efforts were in vain. As she was about to give up, she heard Ben's voice.

"Hey there, what are you doing?"

She was bent over leaning into the backseat with her bottom in the air. She tried to quickly exit backward out of the backseat and bumped her head on the door frame. "Ouch," she muttered, now standing and rubbing the back of her head.

Ben looked at her with concern and asked, "Are you okay?"

Embarrassed and flushed, she replied, "No, not really." Then, her eyes watered, and she couldn't stop the erupting tears.

Ben leaned in close to her and started to examine her head.

She shook her head and said, "No, it's not that. My head is fine. Sorry, I feel like I'm an emotional mess right now. I'm a little overwhelmed trying to juggle everything. I'm upset about so many things, but I'm trying to be strong. I think my strength is dwindling."

Ben immediately pulled her into his arms without thinking. He wanted to hold her and to comfort her. It hurt him to see her like this. It felt good to have her body close to his, and he wanted to make everything okay for her. She responded to him and burrowed her head into his chest. Delaney felt a wave of stress and tightness leave her body. Ben's arms made her world feel right again, and she wanted to stay there forever.

After a moment of silence, Ben loosened his hold and stepped back to look at her. He asked, "What is your daughter's name?"

She responded, as she wiped the wetness off her cheeks, "Gracie Elyse."

"That's beautiful. I can't wait to meet her," he whispered.

She looked up at him and smiled. Ben looked over her shoulder into the car. He gently moved Delaney to the side and said, "Let me help with this."

Delaney shook her head, "There must be some kind of magic needed to put that thing in. I can't do it."

He smiled at her and replied, "There's a trick to it."

Within five minutes, the car seat was installed. Delaney was amazed at how quickly he had accomplished the task. She said, "This may be small to you, but your help today has been huge. Thank you."

"It's just a car seat. No big deal," he replied with a chuckle.

"No," she said. "I'm not talking about that. I mean, I'm thankful you worked your magic on the car seat, but I'm talking about your encouragement today. Thank you for just being here."

Ben pursed his lips and nodded. "I'm sure everything will work out."

After a quick goodbye, Delaney got into her car and drove off. Ben baffled her. One moment, he could be so aloof and distant, and in the next, he could swallow her up in his arms as if she belonged with him. Her heart ached for him, and she didn't know how to stop it.

Chapter 24

A s she drove to the south hospital, her cell phone rang. "Dang it," she muttered, thinking it was another surgical patient or a patient in labor. She just wanted to get back to Gracie.

"Hey, Delaney. I hear congratulations are in order," said Griffin.

Delaney was relieved to hear it was Griffin. "Oh hey, Griffin. Yes, thank you. Her name is Gracie Elyse, and I'll be bringing her home tomorrow. She's really perfect. I feel so blessed."

"Well, I'm very happy for you. I'm also calling because I have some good news for you. I found a doctor by the name of Dwight Brown to start covering your call on weekends and evenings, through next Sunday morning. He can start right now. Do you have anything going on that you need to tell him about?" he asked.

"Really? That's so awesome. Thank you so much," she exclaimed. Then, she added, "I just finished a surgery for an ectopic pregnancy, but that's it. There is no one in labor."

"Enjoy your new baby. All you have to do is cover office next week. Dr. Brown will cover the rest until next Sunday," said Griffin. Then, he added, "Dr. Brown is a friend of mine from Birmingham. I'll give him your number in case he has any questions."

Delaney felt relieved. "Thank you, Griffin. This is great news. I can't tell you how much I appreciate this right now." They disconnected the call. Delaney smiled with contentment. Now, she could feel more at peace without having to worry about night coverage, at least for the next week.

Delaney and Gracie headed home the following day. As Delaney strapped Gracie into her car seat for the first time, she couldn't help but think of Ben, since his hands had been on the car seat installing it just the day before. She recalled him taking her into his arms and holding her, just when she was at her breaking point. She hadn't wanted him to let go. She found herself wanting to share her joy over Gracie with Ben, but she knew he couldn't handle it.

Delaney cancelled her office patients on Monday and then took Gracie with her to the office for the rest of the week. She was glad she had set up a nursery in her office. Candace and the other ladies in the office were more than happy to take turns holding and watching Gracie. Delaney was able to see all of the patients without much interruption. Although she took several breaks every couple of hours to hold Gracie and feed her and love on her, she was still able to manage the patient load.

Delaney exhaled Friday night when she pulled into her driveway. Gracie had been crying when Delaney's car pulled out of the parking lot at work, but the car ride had lulled her to sleep within a few minutes. The 15-minute drive home was quiet and gave Delaney's developing migraine a break. She felt exhausted. The week had been long, even minus the Monday office. Gracie had been up every two to three hours every night, which had started to wear on Delaney by Wednesday. It didn't help that she felt obligated to watch Gracie sleep most of the time for fear that she would wake up choking or stop breathing. The women at work told Delaney she was having normal, new mommy fears. Delaney wondered how other single moms managed. She knew she couldn't keep up this pace. She had to find a babysitter as soon as possible. Monday was coming up, and she was going to be back on call coverage. She didn't want to have to bring Gracie into the hospital with her for deliveries or surgeries.

After only a few minutes inside, Gracie woke up and began wailing. Delaney changed her wet diaper and prepared a bottle for her. She took one of her migraine pills and then sat down in the rocking chair with Gracie. As soon as the bottle entered Gracie's little mouth, the wailing crisis was over. Delaney exhaled and laid her head back on the chair. She kicked off the boots she had worn with her black dress slacks. The room was quiet and dark, which is what her head needed right now. Delaney thought about the day. Today had been especially hectic for some reason. She opened her eyes when she realized she hadn't even finished her first cup of coffee that morning. "Caffeine withdrawal headache," she whispered, rolling her eyes. She wondered how many other things she had forgotten. She burped Gracie and then lay her down in her crib. She seemed content, as she made a few cute, cooing noises and then settled into a deep sleep. Delaney leaned down and kissed her cheek gently.

In the kitchen, Delaney got out the French press pot and then looked through the pantry for some coffee beans. She felt deflated, as she realized she was out of coffee. She sighed heavily with the pounding in her head growing louder. As she searched some more, she thought she heard a faint knock at the door. She listened and then heard it again. She walked toward the front door and could see it was dark outside. She hadn't had time to turn on the front porch light yet. She flipped the light on and opened the door. She was surprised to see Ben standing there with what looked like a bag of groceries.

"Hi, I hope I'm not bothering you," he said.

Delaney could feel her eyes light up and her heart jump in her chest, "No, not at all. Please, come in."

Ben stepped in out of the cold and said, "I didn't want to ring the doorbell and wake up Gracie. I'm here because I figured you might need a few groceries and some dinner. Everyone at the hospital has been talking about your nursery at the office. We all know you're having a tough time."

"You are so kind, Ben. Thank you. I just put Gracie in her crib, and she's sleeping. I am starving and in need of caffeine, and my head hurts. So I apologize ahead of time if I'm a terrible hostess," she said with that new mommy face of exhaustion.

Ben smiled at her and said, "Well, if you don't mind, I'll make my way to the kitchen and try to fix your ailments."

Delaney managed a chuckle, despite her pounding headache. "C'mon in," she said and motioned for him to follow her to the kitchen.

Ben could see the fatigue in her face, and he knew her head was hurting just by looking at her eyes. Despite that, she still looked beautiful. She was still in her work clothes. She had on black, fitted dress slacks that accented her slender figure. Her medium green blouse brought out the olive in her eyes. "Listen," he said. "Direct me to your French press and a pot that I can warm up soup in and then go lie down. I'll bring dinner to you."

"Oh, I can't lie down. I have too much to do. I need to sterilize Gracie's bottles. She will need to eat in an hour," she said, holding her temple.

"No, I've got this. I know how to sterilize bottles. Go lie down. It's an order. I will make dinner and listen for Gracie," Ben replied.

Delaney's eyes started to water, but she fought back the tears. She had cried the last time he saw her, and she couldn't cry again. She couldn't believe he was here now and wondered how he seemed to know when she was at the brink of exhaustion. Why was he here? Maybe he really did just care. She was too tired, and her head hurt too much to think about it anymore. She just nodded her head and said, "Thank you, Ben. I'll be on the couch." Delaney flipped the fireplace on and then fell asleep within minutes.

Chapter 25

A bout an hour later, she awoke to the sound of Gracie's cry. She jumped up from the couch not knowing what day it was. She stood confused for a moment and then remembered it was Friday night, and Ben had come over. Her head felt better, and whatever was cooking in the kitchen smelled wonderful. The aroma of fresh coffee lured her toward the kitchen. The lights were still on, but she didn't see Ben. She assumed he had left. Gracie stopped crying, and Delaney darted toward the nursery. When she got to the doorway, the light was on, and Ben was picking Gracie up from the changing table.

"She had a full diaper, and now her little tummy is ready for food," he said.

Delaney rubbed her eyes to make sure she was seeing this right. Ben was holding Gracie out in front of him talking to her. She was sucking on her fist and cooing. Delaney was speechless. She hadn't thought he'd want to go anywhere near a baby, but here he was doing baby talk. Delaney smiled and said, "Thank you, Ben," and she reached for Gracie.

"You can hold her for a minute, but your dinner is waiting in the kitchen. I want you to eat. I'll feed the pretty girl," he said, cooing at Gracie.

"Well, okay. Are you sure? I can feed her first ..." Delaney started.

Ben interrupted her, "I'm sure. You need to eat, too. I have your food ready. The soup is warming in the pot on the stove, the rolls are warming in the oven, and I just made fresh coffee. I will be very upset if you let my hard work go to waste. Eat it while it's warm."

Delaney smiled at him, and they headed to the kitchen. Delaney handed Gracie to Ben and said, "I'll get her bottle ready and bring it to you. Then, I'll eat my dinner as ordered."

Ben seemed satisfied with that and motioned by nodding his head toward the living room. "We will be in here next to the fire reclining in the chair."

Ben and Gracie disappeared into the living room. Delaney prepared a bottle and took it in to him. She returned to the kitchen and prepared a bowl of the potato soup and a cup of coffee with cream and sugar. She put a roll on a plate and then decided to put her dinner on a serving tray.

Ben sat quietly holding Gracie's bottle in her mouth. He hadn't held a baby for years, not since—stopped his thoughts. Instead, he focused on her little features. She had a little button nose and her tiny lips were working hard on the bottle. He was surprised by how much hair she had. He couldn't believe a newborn could have so many brown, curly locks. She almost looked as if she had a miniature wig on. She was just beautiful. She stopped drinking her bottle for a moment and looked up at him. He pulled the bottle back, as she tried to focus on him. He started talking to her in a sweet whisper, "Hi, pretty girl. Hi, pretty girl."

As Delaney turned the corner to walk into the living room carrying her serving tray, she could see Ben cradling Gracie and feeding her. He was talking to her in a gentle whisper. Her heart ached at the sight of them together. Ben looked up when he saw her come into the room.

"I think it's time for a burp," he said.

"You're a natural, Ben," she said.

Ben didn't say anything as he put Gracie up on his chest and started patting her back. He looked as if he belonged with her, as if he should be her daddy. The natural bond was evident. She could imagine coming home to him every day and could see him being Gracie's daddy. She could see him as the man in her life, as her husband. Her face flushed as she realized how strong her feelings had become for him. She wanted him to stay with them, with her, and be part of their lives every day. He made her feel safe and cared for and that she belonged. This was something she hadn't felt for a long time. After the loss of her parents, she had lost all sense of family and of belonging anywhere. She had hoped her place would be with Pierce, at one point, but he had only left her feeling betrayed and more alone.

Ben looked at Delaney and caught her staring at him. She was glad the lights were dim in the room, because she knew her face was scarlet. She was yearning for this man holding her child. She ate her dinner after taking a few big swigs of her coffee. "Mmmm, this is so delicious. I feel like I haven't eaten for days."

"I'm glad you're enjoying it," replied Ben. Then, he added, "I figured you didn't have time to take care of yourself, so I wanted to be sure someone was taking care of you."

His words surprised her, and she looked up at him again. For a moment, their eyes locked. He was that someone taking care of her. Her face heated again when she realized the impact of his words. He was concerned about her. Before now, she wasn't sure. He had been so hot and cold so far. She knew he had haunting memories, but she had started to believe that maybe he just didn't care for her enough.

He stood from the chair holding Gracie and asked, "Is it okay if I put her in her crib? She's asleep. Don't worry, she let out a good burp before she went to sleep."

Delaney stood and walked with him to the nursery. Ben laid Gracie in her crib on her side. Delaney checked the monitor, and then, they headed back to the living room.

Ben looked at her empty bowl and said, "You were hungry, weren't you?"

"Yes, and I think I still have room for dessert," she chuckled.

"Well, do you like apple pie?" he asked.

"Yes, I love it," she said, nodding her head.

"I brought you one. It's still in the bag," he said smiling at her.

Delaney's expression went from one of happy surprise to a big smile. She shook her head.

"What?" he asked with a big grin on his face.

"You are too good to me. You're a keeper for sure. I think Gracie agrees," she replied. "Want some pie and coffee?"

Ben held an expression that seemed pained for a moment, and then, he half smiled and said, "Sure, sounds great."

Ben followed Delaney to the kitchen. He found a couple of plates and forks, while Delaney made some more coffee. They sat down at the kitchen table and ate the pie. There was an awkward silence. After a few moments of silence, Ben had finished his pie. He leaned back in his chair, and his affect had changed again. He pushed back from the table and stood. "I've got to be going," he said.

Delaney felt disappointment. "Are you sure? We could watch a movie?"

"No," he said gruffly. "You need rest, and I need to get home."

What had she said? Why did this sudden coldness come over him? Delaney stood and said, "Okay, you're right. I'm pretty tired. Thank you for your help tonight. I'm not sure how I would have managed without you."

"You're one of the strongest women I've ever met. I know you would have done fine. I just wanted to give you a break. I remember how hard the first few weeks can be with a newborn." His face showed pain with those words, as if he was thinking of his daughter.

They stood motionless by the kitchen table. Ben seemed lost in thought, while Delaney stared at him. She placed her hand on his arm, wanting to tell him she understood his pain. He turned his eyes toward her. Her touch sent electricity through his body. He pulled her to him and kissed her tenderly on the lips. Then, he held her tightly. Delaney slowly let go of any apprehension or nervousness and wrapped her arms tighter around his neck. This man was incredible in every way, and there was no way she wasn't in love with him.

The sound of Gracie's cries caused Ben and Delaney to loosen their embrace. Ben pulled away and stared at her for a moment. He had that hurting look in his face again, but this time, he looked as if he'd just done something wrong. "I'm sorry about the kiss. I should go," he said.

"No," said Delaney, as she leaned into him, trying to keep her arms around his neck. "It's okay."

"No, it's not. I shouldn't have done that," he said as he gently took her arms and pushed her away. "I can't do this, Delaney," he said with an expression of torment. He rushed past her, and in a moment, he was gone.

Delaney tried to regroup long enough to go pick up Gracie. Her heart ached, and her pulse was still racing from his kiss. What had happened? She methodically changed Gracie's diaper and took her to the kitchen to prepare a bottle. She returned to the nursery and sat down in the rocking chair to feed Gracie. She stared at her sweet baby and watched her eat. Ben was tormented for sure. She knew he had feelings for her. She knew at least part of him enjoyed being with her and Gracie. She wished he could let go of the past, but she knew this wasn't something she could help him with.

A tear ran down her face, as she realized how much pain his hot and cold fits of emotion were causing her. "I can't do this anymore," she whispered. She looked up toward the ceiling and said, "Lord, why is this happening?" She sat there and rocked Gracie until her bottle was empty. After a good burp, Gracie was asleep again. Delaney lay her in her crib and then headed to the kitchen. It was a mess. She felt exhausted physically and emotionally. Her heart was aching, but she couldn't allow herself to be manipulated by Ben's on-and-off feelings for her anymore. She turned the light off, locked the front door, and headed to bed.

131

Chapter 26

Through his streaming tears, Ben tried to focus on the road. He felt like a coward for running out of Delaney's house. He hadn't planned on kissing her. He thought he'd be stronger by now. She made him feel needy, and he didn't want to feel that way. Without his knowledge, she had captured his heart. Gracie was an angel, and he loved holding her and feeding her. He wanted to be there for both of them, but he couldn't betray the memory of Danna and Ella. He had never loved two people more in his life, but now, he knew he was in love with Delaney. Though he wanted to be with her, and he felt a tug on his heart from Gracie, he just couldn't dishonor the memory of his loving wife and child. He had tried, but it was just no good. He wouldn't be able to live with himself. He didn't feel free. "Poorly done," he muttered, feeling ashamed of himself.

At home, he paced his living room floor. The torment was too much. He picked up the framed photograph of Danna and Ella and held it to his chest. He fell to his knees and then lay on the floor sobbing. He cried out, "Lord, I can't take this pain. I feel like I'm grieving Danna and Ella all over again. I'm in love with Delaney. My heart aches to be with her and Gracie, but I don't know how to let go of my past. Please help me. Show me what to do."

Ben lay on the floor for a long time. Eventually, the tears subsided, and he felt exhaustion set in. He slowly rose to his feet and replaced the photograph on the fireplace mantle. He fell across his bed and was asleep within minutes.

The next morning, Ben awoke early before sunrise. He was still in his clothes, and the events of the previous evening lay heavily on his heart. He made coffee and sat outside on his front porch. It was cold, but at least, there was no wind. He took his last sip of coffee, as the sun was just starting to peek over the horizon.

He put his coffee mug away and grabbed a heavier coat, a hat, and gloves. He prepared a thermos of hot coffee, grabbed his Bible, and then headed down to the dock. He needed some peace and felt desperate to have it. The water was very still as Ben took the boat out on the lake. He killed the motor and dropped an anchor. The fog was heavy and swirling around him, and the sun was starting to show itself more now. Ben stared out over the lake as the sun slowly lighted the morning sky. He could see hues of pink and yellow now. He opened his Bible when there was enough light to see and started reading. After a while, he closed his Bible and started to pray, "Lord, please show me what to do. Please give me a sign. I need your help, Lord, please."

Ben opened his eyes and saw the sunrise again. He was astonished as the colors had changed to a beautiful blend of pink and blue. "Lavender sky," he whispered. Peace came over him, as he acknowledged that God was showing him the sky he had shown Delaney many times before. She had told him that her mother had explained that a lavender sky meant good things were to come. In that moment, he knew God was telling him that everything would be okay. He read his Bible a little longer and finished off the thermos of coffee before he headed back home. He felt at ease knowing God was going to take care of this, though he still wasn't sure how. He just knew that he could trust Him.

When he returned home, he decided to text Delaney so he wouldn't awaken Gracie. He hadn't liked the way he had run out the night before. It hadn't been fair to Delaney.

He texted, "Good morning. I thought about you all night. I'm so sorry for the way I ran out. It was wrong of me. I'm struggling with some things right now. I hope you can be patient with me."

Delaney was surprised by his early text. She had slept into the morning out of necessity. Gracie had kept her up for most of night. Delaney texted back, "I can only imagine what you are going through. I wish I could help you more. The problem is that I've fallen in love with you. If I wasn't texting right now, I probably wouldn't be brave enough to say this. I appreciate what you've done for me and Gracie, but I have to ask you to stop coming over. I feel like I'm riding an emotional roller coaster with you. One minute, your heart is open to me, and the next minute, you're so closed off that you completely shut me out. I have to get off this ride now. I have too much turmoil in life to add more to it. Plus, I have to think about Gracie too. Please understand."

Ben's heart felt heavy. She was in love with him, but she was tired of shouldering his emotional wounds. He understood and didn't blame her, but it hurt deeply. He stared at her text for a while. He kept reading the words, "I've fallen in love with you." Then, he said out loud, "I'm in love with you too, Delaney Bartlett." He laid his phone down without replying. That was it then. He looked out the window. The sun was high in the sky now and the fog had burned off. The water was still calm. "So, is this it, Lord?" He asked. "I guess this door is closed," he added, though the words didn't sit right in his gut.

Chapter 27

O n Monday, Delaney and Gracie headed to the office. She wasn't sure how she was going to manage being on call with Gracie in tow that night. As she settled into her office, Candace knocked on the door.

"Good morning, Dr. Bartlett," she said with her usual happy energy.

Delaney cracked a smile, which actually hurt. She realized her heartache over Ben hadn't allowed her to smile much all weekend. "Hi, Candace," she replied.

"I thought I'd stop in for some Gracie time." She reached into the crib and picked up the sleeping baby. "I brought some muffins in, if you're hungry."

"Thanks, Candace. That was thoughtful. I think I'll go get one. I could use some coffee, too."

Delaney headed to the kitchen for a cup of coffee and a muffin. Her cell phone rang, and it was labor and delivery. Her heart sank at the thought of having to go to the hospital now for a delivery.

"Hello?" She answered.

"Hey, Dr. B. This is Krissy," she said.

"Hey, Krissy. How are you?" Delaney asked.

"I'm good. I just wanted to ask ya if you've found a babysitter for Gracie yet?" she asked.

"No, I haven't," she replied.

"Well, I wanted to run something by ya. I talked to Bryan last night, and I asked him what he thought about me cutting back at work, maybe just weekends, so I could watch Gracie at home during the week. He loved the idea. Would ya like me to watch her during the weekdays for ya?"

Delaney exhaled, "Are you serious?"

"Yeah, totally," she replied.

Delaney was ecstatic and asked, "Oh my gosh, lady. When can you start?"

Krissy laughed and said, "I should be able to start within a few days. I've already talked to my boss about it."

Delaney said, "Yes, yes, please. Name your salary. I'm so relieved and thankful."

Krissy chuckled again, "Okay, I'll come up with a fair compensation and get back to ya later today. I'll know my start day soon. I'm so excited."

Delaney disconnected the call and smiled. She looked out the window toward the sky and said, "An answered prayer. Thank you, God."

Her cell phone chirped as she was finishing her muffin. It was Savannah.

"Hey, Dr. B. How are you? I know you tried sending me some pics of Gracie, but I wasn't ready. Would you please start sending them now? How is she doing?"

Delaney was glad to hear from her. She texted, "Of course, I will. I have several saved up for you already. Gracie is doing well. I'm adjusting to her schedule finally. She actually slept four hours straight last night for the first time. I've been thinking about you a lot and praying for you. How are you?"

Savannah replied, "Great to hear you are both adjusting. I remember how hard it is to be up with them all night. I've missed you. I just wanted to say hello and ask you to send me pictures when you get a chance. No hurry. I know how busy you are."

Delaney texted, "I've missed you too. We can get together when you're ready. Here are some pics for you." Delaney sent several photos from her phone.

"She's growing so fast. She's so beautiful. Thank you," Savannah texted.

"She takes after her mama," Delaney sent back.

"You are her mama … though she does take after her birth mom a bit," Savannah replied with a winking emoji.

Delaney sent a smiley face and said, "I'll catch up with you soon. Please stay in touch."

Savannah sent back a smiley face.

Delaney exhaled. It was good to hear from Savannah. She seemed to be adjusting well, and this gave Delaney comfort. Delaney's cell phone rang, and she thought Savannah might be calling to tell her something.

"Hello?"

"Good morning, Delaney. How's the new mommy doing?" Griffin asked.

"Oh, hey, Griffin. I'm great. It's good to hear from you. Any news for me?" She asked.

"Well, I thought you might want to know that Finn has entered rehab. He's going to be there for at least three months, if not more. I just thought you would want to know he's getting the help he needs. I know you two are good friends. Also, I don't have any more information about the investigation."

"That is really good news. I have been thinking about him and praying that he gets the help he needs," said Delaney.

"Another bit of good news is that he and his wife have decided to fight for their marriage. They are both getting the help they need as individuals, and then, they'll start marriage counseling together. I'm sure they will need our prayers as they both try to move forward," Griffin said.

"It's good to hear that they will be fighting together," Delaney responded. She silently wished someone else she knew and loved could move forward with his life.

"On another note, I think I've recruited a doctor to join you," he said.

Delaney's face lit up and she replied, "You're just full of good news this morning. I'm so glad to hear from you. So who is this doctor, and when can he or she start?"

"Well, it's Dr. Brown, my friend who has already covered some call. We just need to put him through the employment and credentialing process. I figured you might also want to meet him first," he said.

"The sooner the better. I'm ready for him to start yesterday," she replied.

"Okay. Well, we can get the administrative paperwork done within a week. I'll bring him by to meet you later this week," he said.

"That's wonderful news. Thank you so much, Griffin," she replied, grinning from ear-to-ear. Delaney let out a big sigh. Things were starting to fall into place. The only missing link was one that was connected to her heart, but Ben had already told her he couldn't be the one she needed. She dismissed that thought and, instead, decided to thank God for all the good things coming her way. Her only task now would be finding someone to help her with Gracie during her night call. That would be tricky.

Chapter 28

After work, Delaney and Gracie headed home. It had been a very long Monday for both of them. Gracie seemed a little more fussy than usual, and Delaney knew the interruptions in her sleep schedule had contributed. She couldn't wait for Krissy to start watching her. Gracie needed a set schedule with one care-taker during the day. Delaney also wanted to get Gracie away from a medical environment. She had seen a few patients with the flu lately, and Delaney felt like a bad mom for potentially exposing Gracie to germs. She had adhered to strict handwashing rules for the ladies at the office, but she knew how sneaky germs could be. It would be good to be able to take Gracie to Krissy's house during the day.

Delaney put Gracie in her crib after she fell asleep. Delaney retreated to the kitchen and prepared a pot of coffee. She proceeded to grab a bite to eat, start some laundry, and then clean the kitchen. She couldn't subdue the anxiety she felt about being called to the hospital. She didn't have anyone to watch Gracie. She was going to have to figure something out soon.

She flipped on the fireplace and decided to watch one of her favorite movies, *Facing the Giants*. It seemed to be her go-to flick when she needed encouragement. She lay back in the recliner, and thoughts of Ben surfaced. The situation with him seemed hopeless. She worried that he would never be able to commit himself to her fully, because Danna would always be there, taking up space in his heart. She could understand, but she was also jealous of Danna's hold on him, even beyond the grave. He had really loved her, and he and Danna must have had an incredible relationship. Even if he could find some way to open his heart to Delaney, she felt that she would always be competing with Danna. Her eyes collected tears, as the hopelessness of that possibility flooded her soul.

Delaney's cell phone rang and awakened her. She raised her head up from the recliner to answer her phone. She had fallen asleep, and her movie had ended.

"Hello?"

"Hey, Dr. B. It's Krissy. Sorry to bug ya, but a Hispanic patient just showed up in labor. It's her third baby, and she's already eight centimeters dilated."

Delaney exhaled loudly and stood up from the recliner. "Well, okay. I'll get there as soon as I can, and I have to bring Gracie with me."

"No problem, Dr. B. I can watch her. Just please drive safely. I asked Dr. Paine in the ER to be on standby. I think she's going to deliver soon," said Krissy.

"Okay, I'm on my way," said Delaney.

Delaney looked at the time. It was 2:00 a.m. She had anticipated this scenario several times already. So it wasn't a surprise that a patient was in labor, but it made her feel really mad at Finn right now. If his situation had not happened, she would have had more time to prepare for Gracie and to arrange for proper on-call care for her.

She hurried to Gracie's room and put her in her little snowsuit. Luckily, Delaney had decided to sleep in scrubs, so she only had to brush her teeth and slip on her shoes. She strapped Gracie into her car seat and pulled out of the driveway. There was no snow on the ground, but the weather had been uncharacteristically cold for Alabama. Tonight, the temperature had hovered at freezing.

Delaney drove as quickly as she could without being reckless. She knew she had to protect the precious cargo onboard. She turned out of her neighborhood and drove onto the Lake Guntersville Bridge. At the bottom of the bridge, she decided to turn right and drive along the lake, since it was a shorter distance to the hospital. She expected Krissy to call her any minute and tell her that the patient had already delivered. She felt stressed and frustrated again at the fact that she was having to bring Gracie in with her. Thankfully, Gracie didn't seem to mind and continued to sleep.

Within about one mile of the hospital, Delaney passed a wooded area. She glanced down at the time for a second, and when she looked back up, a deer had darted right in front of her. Terror struck her as she slammed on her brakes and tried to make a controlled swerve away from the animal. She felt her SUV sliding, and then, she heard a screech and a loud thump. Her airbag deployed as her car came to a stop, and her engine died. She sat there for a few minutes feeling dazed.

From a distance, she could hear a baby crying. Delaney shook her head and tried to concentrate. Her awareness seemed to be returning, and she realized it was Gracie that was wailing. She looked around in the car to get her bearings. "Ouch," she groaned as she tried to move her neck. The airbag was partially deflated in front of her face. Her purse contents had spilled onto the floor, and her knees hurt. She grimaced and then realized her face and chest were also sore. She slowly moved different parts of her body to be sure she was intact. Then, she tried to open her car door, but it was jammed. She needed to get to Gracie but couldn't. "Lord, please let her be okay," she cried out. She was shaking as tears erupted. She looked up to the heavens and cried out for help. As she did, she could see blue lights in her rearview mirror. "Thank you, Lord," she whispered.

A police officer appeared at her window. He pulled the door hard and was able to open it. "Are you okay, ma'am?"

Delaney looked toward him engulfed in panic, "I'm fine. I hit a deer. My baby is in the backseat. Is she okay? Please get her now."

"Okay, just don't move. I will get her." The officer opened the backseat door and removed the unharmed car seat from its base. He said, "She looks unharmed. I have an ambulance on the way. Are you hurt?"

"I don't think anything is broken, and I'm not having a lot of pain, except in my neck and my knees. I'm just sore," she replied.

"Can you give me your name and tell me what are you doing out at this hour, ma'am?" The officer asked.

"My name is Delaney Bartlett. I'm an OB doctor, and I was on my way to deliver a baby at the hospital," she replied.

"With your newborn in the car?" he asked.

Delaney felt irritated with his line of questioning and replied, "Believe me when I say that I had no choice."

The officer seemed to accept that answer. By then, a few other people had stopped to see if they could be of some assistance, and then, the ambulance arrived.

The EMS crew removed Delaney from the car on a stretcher and put a cervical collar on her to protect her neck. Then, they went system by system to verify that her injuries did not appear life-threatening. With tears in her eyes, she demanded to see Gracie.

After the EMS worker examined Gracie, he held her up beside Delaney and said, "Ma'am, my name is Micah, and your daughter seems to be fine. How are you doing?" Gracie was no longer wailing and seemed to be content in his arms.

"I'm fine. I'm just glad she is okay," replied Delaney.

The other EMS worker loaded Delaney into the ambulance, and then, Micah sat in the back beside her holding Gracie next to her. Delaney reached out for Gracie and held onto her telling her that mommy was right there. As the officer started to close the back doors, Delaney called out, "Officer!"

"Yes, ma'am," he answered.

Can you please call this number, 555-2289. It's the number to labor and delivery. Please tell them what's happened to me. They're going to wonder why I'm not there yet."

"I'll take care of it right now," he answered.

Chapter 30

••••••••••••

U pon arrival to the ER, Delaney and Gracie were taken to the trauma room. Dr. Paine appeared and was shocked to see Delaney.

"I heard what happened. Are you hurting anywhere?" he asked.

"Doc, please just check out Gracie first. I'm okay," she pleaded with him.

He replied, "Sure thing."

Doc laid Gracie on a stretcher beside Delaney so she could watch him examine her. He carefully pulled Gracie from her snowsuit. Gracie screamed loudly in response to being exposed to the chilly ER air. Doc did a quick check of her systems and said, "Delaney, she looks great. She's kicking and screaming and just wants her clothes back on. We'll watch her overnight, since you need to stay. Don't worry, you'll be able to stay with her."

Delaney exhaled a sigh of relief, "Thank you so much, Doc."

He turned to her, "Now, where are you hurting? I know the airbag deployed, and you mentioned your knees to the EMS crew."

"Yes," she said. "My face, neck, and chest hurt and my knees. I think I hit my knees on the dash."

Doc did a careful exam and then ordered several tests. He said, "I know you understand how this goes, but I need to order several tests and some imaging to make sure you didn't break anything and to make sure you have no internal injuries."

Delaney replied, "That's fine, but would you get my neck imaging done first, so I can get this collar off and hold Gracie?"

"Absolutely," he replied.

"Oh my gosh!" Krissy exclaimed peeking out from behind Doc, as she entered the room. "What happened, Dr. B? Are ya okay? I just heard. I got worried when I couldn't reach ya on your phone, and then, the police officer called me and told me what happened. I've been sick with worry."

Doc interrupted Krissy and relayed the events of the accident. Then, he added, "Gracie is fine, and I think Dr. B is going to be fine too.

"I'm so glad you're both okay. Your poor face is so bruised. That airbag did a number on you." Then, she added, "I'm going to stay here with you and Gracie tonight. I can take care of Gracie."

"Thank you, Krissy," Delaney said as she closed her eyes, feeling relieved. She knew there was no one else to help her. She was grateful for Krissy.

"Now don't fall asleep," said Doc. "I need you to stay awake for a while."

"I'm fine. I won't go to sleep. I'm just relieved that Krissy can help me with Gracie, but I do suddenly feel tired. This has been too much."

Delaney didn't want to cry, but she couldn't help it. The accident had been surreal, like a bad dream. When she had first come out of her daze, she had heard Gracie crying. She couldn't imagine what she would have done if something had happened to her. She thought of Ben and started to really understand how hard it had to have been to lose the two people in the world who mattered to him so much. She couldn't bear the thought of Gracie being injured, much less dying. Ben had been through something so terrible. She cried more as she grieved for him.

After Delaney underwent a few x-rays and CT scans, Doc came in and removed her cervical collar. "Your spine has been cleared, so we can take this off," he said.

"Thank God," she said. Doc helped her sit up, and she immediately held out her arms for Gracie.

Krissy eagerly put Gracie in her arms and said, "She's hungry. I'll go get some formula and diapers from the nursery. I haven't found your diaper bag yet, but here is your purse."

Delaney nodded but didn't speak, as she stared into the eyes of her sweet baby. Holding her was all she had wanted to do since the accident. It felt so good to finally cradle Gracie in the safety of her arms. She kissed her cheek over and over. "Thank you, Lord," she whispered.

Doc returned in a few minutes. "Well, you have a few small contusions on your face and chest from the airbag, and your knees are bruised pretty badly, but everything seems to be intact. You're one lucky lady." Then, he chuckled and said, "The deer didn't fare so well, though, and you owe me for the delivery of one baby."

Delaney had forgotten about the delivery. Her eyes widened as she looked up at Doc and said, "Oh, I forgot all about the patient in labor. How did the delivery go?"

Doc smiled, "It was very straightforward, and it counted toward my delivery number, which was very helpful. Though, the next time you want me to do a delivery, just call and ask me. You don't have to hit a deer."

Delaney held her side and laughed, "Oh, that hurt. Don't make me laugh."

He replied, "It's good to hear you laugh. I'm so glad you are both okay."

"Thanks, Doc," she replied. "I know God was watching over us."

Chapter 31

D elaney and Gracie were moved out of the ER later that night to a room on the fifth floor. Gracie was asleep in Krissy's arms, and Delaney had just started to rest when she heard commotion in the hallway outside her room.

Delaney heard the nurse say, "Doc, said she needed to rest. Don't go in there and wake her up."

"Sorry, but I have to see them," she faintly heard the reply. It was a man's voice.

Within a few seconds, the door opened, and Ben pushed his way through the doorway. Once he was in the room, he stopped in his tracks, while his eyes searched for Delaney in the dark. When he saw her, he moved slowly to her bedside, as if he was afraid of what he would find. She turned on the bedside light, and she could see the anguish in his eyes.

"Delaney, are you okay?" He glanced to the other side of the bed and saw Krissy holding Gracie. The baby was sleeping comfortably. He exhaled a sigh of relief and moved to sit on the side of the bed.

"I'm fine," Delaney said. "Doc, said I have a few contusions on my face, neck, and chest. And my knees are bruised, but I'm much better than I look. It's just bruising. Gracie is perfectly fine."

He proceeded to carefully look her over and grimaced at seeing her bruised face and chest. "I just found out. I'm sorry I wasn't here sooner."

"Ben, you are not my keeper. I didn't expect you to be here. It's okay."

"No, it's not okay," he said. "I should have been the person you could call, the someone you could depend on."

Krissy stood up and said, "I'm going to take Gracie for a walk in the hall."

Ben walked over to Gracie and kissed her cheek, and then, Krissy disappeared with Gracie into the hallway.

Ben rushed back to Delaney's side. He kneeled down and leaned into her, holding her gently. "I'm so sorry I wasn't here," he said as tears spilled down his face. "I don't know what I would do if anything ever happened to you. Please tell me you really are okay."

Delaney furrowed her brows as she felt the weight of his agony. She knew he had been through a terrible loss when he'd had to say goodbye to his wife and child. It was as if he was reliving the pain. "I'm really okay, Ben. I'll be going home later today."

Ben struggled to his feet and then sat next to her on the bed facing her. "Delaney, I need to tell you something."

Delaney was taken aback by the seriousness in his face. "What is it?" she asked.

Ben took her hands gently in his, and said, "When Danna and Ella were taken from me, I wanted to die. I didn't understand why God would leave me behind, alone, without them. For years, I've felt as if life wasn't worth living. I've begged God to take me many times. I've not been able to feel joy or love or a desire to keep on living, until recently."

Ben paused and looked down at their joined hands. Then, he looked up at her again and said, "When you and Gracie came along, you both slowly opened my heart. I've been afraid to allow myself to fall in love with you and Gracie for fear of losing you, too. So I put up a wall to try to block myself from feeling for you. I've felt so much guilt about dishonoring Danna and Ella, because I want you and Gracie in my life."

Delaney looked at him with kind eyes and shook her head slowly. She said, "You don't have to tell me this. I understand."

Ben shook his head back and forth and said, "No, you don't understand. You see, I need you and Gracie. God has known this all along. I've really been praying about it. In my affliction, I finally asked God to please send me a sign to show me what to do."

Delaney looked at him with anticipation in her face. "Did he give you a sign?" she asked.

Ben paused for a moment and looked away as if he was seeing a memory. He said, "The other day when I was out in my boat on the lake, I saw it."

Delaney furrowed her eyebrows, "You saw what?"

He replied, "A lavender sky."

Delaney exhaled deeply and bowed her head for a moment. When she looked up at Ben, a tear rolled down her face.

"I was too boneheaded to come find you right then and tell you that I'm in love with you," he said.

Delaney tried to hold back more tears, without success, as she inhaled his every word.

"I love you, Delaney, and I love Gracie. I want us to be a family. God is giving me a second chance. I understand what he wants me to do now," he cried.

Delaney nodded and choked out, "I love you, too."

Ben kneeled down on one knee and took Delaney's hand, as Krissy walked back in the room with Gracie sleeping in her arms. Krissy froze at the door. Her eyes and her smile widened as she realized what was happening.

"Delaney Bartlett, will you and Gracie Elyse please marry me and be my family?" Ben asked.

Delaney closed her eyes and uttered a small prayer of thanks to God for her second chance. Then, she opened her eyes, with tears still streaming, and said, "Yes, we would love to."

Ben leaned into Delaney gently and brushed his lips against her. Then, Krissy walked over with tears in her eyes and handed Gracie to Ben.

"Here, Daddy," she said.

Ben sat down on the bed beside Delaney holding Gracie in one arm and Delaney in his other arm. The three of them cuddled as Ben kissed Gracie's cheek. Delaney looked at Ben and kissed him gently. Then, she said, "You are my lavender sky."

Epilogue

D elaney awakened with a sour stomach. She got up and meandered to the kitchen to nibble on some crackers. She must have eaten something bad the night before, she thought. But then again, she'd noticed a sour stomach most mornings for the last week. Coffee didn't sound good, so she knew something wasn't right. She walked into the living room and turned on the fireplace and the Christmas tree lights.

It was still early on Friday morning, and the sun was still slumbering. Delaney had just checked on Gracie, and she was sleeping peacefully in her crib. Delaney removed the framed photo from the mantle in her living room and stared at it. She smiled with warmth filling her heart, as she looked at her wedding photo. It was hard for Delaney to believe that a year had already gone by. Ben had been so handsome in his black tuxedo. She knew she had married the most handsome man in the world, and for a moment, she wondered how she could be so lucky. But then, she knew how.

Delaney had chosen a long, white A-line dress with a lace bodice and sleeves. She had wanted a simple, yet elegant dress. Ben was holding Gracie in her sweet, white dress with ruffles. She had been so little then, only three months old. The flowers and ribbons had been the perfect shade of lavender. White lights had been strewn across the gazebo in Guntersville Park, and the scenery by the lake had added so much beauty.

She recalled that day, as she and Ben took their vows, with Krissy as her matron of honor and Bryan as Ben's best man. Ben's parents had been there, and they had even stayed in town to watch Gracie, while Delaney and Ben honeymooned in Pigeon Forge, Tennessee, the following week. The whole day had been magical, like a dream.

Pastor Buddy from the local Guntersville Christian Church had married them. Even now, Delaney couldn't believe that she had been so blessed. The reception had been hours of bliss for her. There had been good food, fun music, and dancing until the late hours of the night. Delaney recalled all of their friends that had been there to be a part of her and Ben's special day. She couldn't help but cherish this memory over and over.

Delaney looked up to see Ben walking from the bedroom in his pajamas. He walked over to her, smiling, and wrapped her in his arms.

"Good morning, beautiful," he whispered in her ear.

"Good morning, love," she whispered back.

Ben brushed his lips against hers and then stared at the photo she was holding. "Best day of my second chance," he said with a big grin.

"Mine too," she replied, smiling.

"How about some coffee?" he asked.

"You read my mind," she replied.

He smiled at her and then moved toward the kitchen.

After a moment longer, Delaney replaced the photo and joined Ben in the kitchen. She sat quietly at the counter as she waited for the coffee.

"You're quiet this morning," he noticed.

"Today is a special day," she commented.

He smiled at her as he handed her a cup of coffee, "It's hard to believe that I'll officially become Gracie's daddy today. I'm amazed every day at God's goodness to me and to us."

"Me too," she said with a look of contentment, as she took her first sip of the aromatic brew. It didn't taste as good as usual, though, and she felt a wave of nausea pass over her. She looked at Ben and said, "I thought we could go to your lake house for a while today."

"*Our* lake house," he corrected her.

She smiled, "Oh yes, right, *our* lake house. I thought maybe we could bundle up and go out on the lake for a short trip."

Ben raised his eyebrows, "You want to go out on the lake today in this cold?" He had a twinkle in his eye, as he added, "You're not thinking of going for a swim today, are you?"

"Ben Montgomery, that's not even funny," she scolded, pointing her finger at him. They both laughed.

Ben sipped his coffee a few more times and then said, "That's a really great idea. I can't think of a better way to celebrate this day." Ben noticed that Delaney wasn't drinking her coffee. "Are you feeling okay today? You've hardly drunk any of your coffee. That's not like you."

"Oh, I'm fine. I think I'm just a little excited about today," she replied. Delaney looked at the stove clock and said, "We need to be at the courthouse at nine o'clock. I'd better get moving. I'll get myself together and then get Delaney ready."

Ben replied, "Dress her warm. We can go straight out to the lake house after the hearing."

Delaney nodded as she got up from the counter stool. "We don't need to stay out in the boat long. I just think we need to go have a little celebration of today and our lives together. I'll bring some hot chocolate in a thermos."

Ben held Gracie, as he and Delaney sat in the courtroom waiting for the judge. It was an informal hearing, so they sat at a table with their lawyer. Within a few minutes, Judge Albert walked through the door in his jeans and a sweatshirt.

"Mornin'," he said to everyone seated at the table. He sat down, and the lawyer handed him the paperwork.

Judge Albert smiled and said with his thick Southern draw, "Sorry I'm so informal today, but this is an informal hearin'. After this, I'm headin' out to the lake for a day of fishin'. It's been a long time since I've been out there. Supposed to be a pretty day, even though it's a bit on the cold side."

Ben commented, "We're heading out there for a short boat ride today, too. The water looks calm."

The judge looked up at Ben from the paperwork and smiled, "Be sure to take a few blankets and some hot coffee. And if I see y'all out there, don't disturb the fish." Everyone chuckled.

The judge signed the paperwork and then stood from his chair. "Well, congratulations, Daddy. Y'all have a fun day together. Maybe I'll see y'all out at the lake."

Ben and the lawyer stood and shook hands.

Everyone thanked the judge as he turned to leave.

Ben reached for Gracie. He took her in his arms and held her tightly. His face showed a look of gratefulness and joy, as his eyes started to water.

"Da-da," Gracie said as she smacked at his cheeks. She had said the words many times before, but today, they felt official and true.

Delaney observed both of them with a heart full of thankfulness. A little over a year ago, she had been alone, without a husband and without any hope of a family. God had not only forgiven her for her past mistake, but He had also blessed her beyond her imagination. Tears clouded over her eyes, as she wiped them away.

"Let's head to the lake," Ben said.

Delaney agreed, as she felt another wave of nausea come over her. "Ben, let's grab some sandwiches at the Piggly Wiggly. I think I need some food on my stomach," she added.

"Sounds good, babe," he said as they all hopped in his truck and headed down the road.

At the grocery store, Ben carried Gracie and headed to the Deli. Delaney suddenly felt very queasy. "Ben, I'm going to go to the ladies room," she said, darting toward the restrooms.

"Okay, I'll get the sandwiches and meet you in the truck. I'll pick up some snacks for Gracie too," he replied.

Several minutes later, Delaney climbed into the cab of the truck. Ben looked over at her and asked, "Are you okay? You look a little green."

Delaney mustered a smile and said, "I think I'm just hungry."

"Well, go ahead and eat your sandwich now," he said, as he drove out of the parking lot onto the road.

Gracie sat happily in the backseat in her car seat babbling and chewing on her teething ring. Occasionally, Delaney could make out a "ma-ma" or "da-da" in what she was saying.

Delaney bit into her sandwich feeling ravenous, and by the time they reached the lake, she was feeling much better.

Ben loaded everything into the boat, and then, Delaney climbed in first. Ben handed Gracie to her, protected in her infant life preserver, and then jumped in. He guided the boat to a spot that had become their favorite over the last year. It was in a small narrowing part of the lake with some tree cover. There were no leaves at this time of year, but the tree branches still cast a small roof over this part of the lake. The water was smooth and calm. It was quiet out, since most creatures of nature were hibernating or had gone south for the winter.

Gracie grasped the side of the boat and tried to stand. Her life jacket was bulky, and she complained with irritated sounds to let them know how much she didn't like it. Ben steadied her as he watched her face fill with wonder at her surroundings. The sun had retreated, and the skies were now gray. Thankfully, the lack of a breeze helped keep the cold air at bay.

"Are you feeling better?" Ben asked Delaney.

She smiled at him, "You have no idea how good I feel right now."

He furrowed his eyebrows inferring that he was trying to grasp her meaning. Finally, he smiled and asked, "What do you mean by that?"

Tears came to Delaney's eyes. Ben looked at her with concern. He picked up Gracie and moved to sit in the middle of the boat beside Delaney. "What's wrong? Today is a happy day. You can't cry today. We are together. We have both been given a second chance, and we are a family."

Delaney nodded as she tried to choke back the tears. "I know, and I am happy, but this is also a bittersweet day for me too."

Ben was confused, "What do you mean? Nothing is bitter today, except the cold."

She looked at him and said, "I need to tell you something."

Ben was guarded and seemed worried. "O-k-a-y," he answered, drawing out the word.

Delaney shook her head, "No, it's something from my past that I need to get out. It's something I've held as a secret for so long because I was ashamed. I still am, but I need to tell you about it. I don't want us to have secrets, and there is a reason I need to tell you about it now."

Ben and Gracie were both quiet and looked at Delaney. Gracie studied them both, as if she knew something serious was happening. Ben looked at Delaney and nodded, while he waited for her to speak.

Delaney proceeded to tell Ben about her abortion when she was a teenager. She sobbed as she relived the memory of the procedure and the torment she had endured every day after it. She explained to him how she knew God had forgiven her, but she had struggled to this day to forgive herself. Even with the gift of Gracie, she had still struggled to feel worthy.

Ben wrapped his free arm around Delaney as he held Gracie. "Darling, you have to forgive yourself. Just look at how blessed you are. If you need to hear me say it, I don't judge you. You did what you thought you had to do at the time. You had no one to turn to for help or advice."

Delaney replied, "Well, today, I forgive myself and move forward. I feel certain that God wants me to live my life taking care of the ones He has entrusted to me."

Ben smiled, "So what changed today, the adoption?"

Delaney smiled, "Yes, and there's more."

Been raised both eyebrows in anticipation of her next comment.

"You're a daddy today in more ways than one," she said.

Ben shook his head and pursed his lips, as he said, "I don't understand." Then, he tilted his head to one side and raised an eyebrow, as he began to understand her meaning.

"I'm pregnant," she said, as a tear of joy rolled down her cheek.

Ben's smile widened with excitement, and his body jerked and caused the boat to rock back and forth. He sat still for a moment to calm the rocking boat and then stared at her. "Are you sure? When did you find out?"

She replied, "Yes, I'm sure. I did a pregnancy test today at the Piggly Wiggly. It was positive. I've been having morning sickness for over a week, but today was the first time I recognized it."

Ben leaned toward Delaney and buried his head in her chest as tears escaped his eyes. Gracie smacked at his hair saying, "Da-da."

Ben and Delaney held each other and Gracie for several minutes. Gracie was growing bored and started reaching to get down.

Delaney looked up to get a better hold of Gracie and saw that Gracie was trying to catch big, fluffy snowflakes in her little hands.

"Ben, look," she said, nudging him to sit upright.

Ben looked up.

"Isn't this beautiful?" Delaney asked with wonder in her eyes.

"Yes, it is," he said, looking directly at Delaney.

"God must love us," she said.

Ben nodded, "Yeah, He really does. Why do you say it like that?"

She looked toward the heavens and said, "Because despite our worst versions of ourselves in the past, He has still given us so much ... a second chance, redemption, hope, a future, and so much love."

About the Author

D enise Janette Bruneau is a wife, mom, doctor, and writer.
She resides in Kentucky with her husband, Mark, and her
three children. She works as an OB hospitalist, homeschools
her youngest daughter, and writes in her spare time. She enjoys deliv-
ering babies, writing, reading, nature walks, and yoga. She is a breast
cancer survivor and loves the Lord with all of her heart.